"I'm staying here until I know

A few seconds passed before she responded, "That's sweet of you but, Kaleb, I've disrupted your life enough already."

"Are you ready to get rid of me?" he asked.

Rylee shook her head. "No, that's not it at all."

"Are you sure?"

"I'm positive, Kaleb. I enjoy your company. Maybe a little too much."

He raised an eyebrow. "Really?"

She met his gaze. "Yes. Kaleb, I like you. To be honest, I didn't want to like you as much as I do."

"Why not?"

"Because we can't afford to be distracted," Rylee stated.

GUARDIAN DEFENDER

JACQUELIN THOMAS

INTRIGUE

Harlequin®
INTRIGUE™

ISBN-13: 978-1-335-59173-9

Guardian Defender

Copyright © 2024 by Jacquelin Thomas

Harlequin Enterprises ULC
22 Adelaide St. West, 41st Floor
Toronto, Ontario M5H 4E3, Canada
www.Harlequin.com

Printed in Lithuania

Jacquelin Thomas is an award-winning, bestselling author with more than fifty-five books in print. When not writing, she is busy catching up on her reading, attending sporting events and spoiling her grandchildren. Jacquelin and her family live in North Carolina.

Books by Jacquelin Thomas

Harlequin Intrigue

Guardian Defender

Love Inspired Cold Case

Evidence Uncovered
Cold Case Deceit

Harlequin Heartwarming

A Family for the Firefighter
Her Hometown Hero
Her Marine Hero
His Partnership Proposal
Twins for the Holidays

Visit the Author Profile page at Harlequin.com.

CAST OF CHARACTERS

Rylee Greenwood—Survived a deadly ambush and motivated to seek justice and vengeance.

Kaleb Stone—Former US marshal turned private security expert who must confront his past while trying to keep Rylee safe.

Nate Stone—Kaleb's brother and business partner.

Brenda Perez—Does this US Marshals' office employee hold answers that could bring down the agency?

Elena Houston—The wife of Stuart Houston, Rylee's deceased partner.

Easton Bennett—The US marshal is determined to protect Rylee at all costs.

John Martin—John's life of sudden luxury seems suspicious. Is he responsible for the leak in the US Marshals' office?

Calderon—Known as the indomitable enforcer of the Mancuso cartel empire.

Poppy Mancuso—The widow of Raul Mancuso navigates a treacherous path as whispers suggest she's inherited the cartel's reins.

Chapter One

Just as she did every time she worked, Rylee gave a cursory scan of the restaurant, checking the tables for any patrons who seemed fixated on her. A party of four waited at the hostess stand, so she took one last look in their direction before moving on to an older couple standing near the bar. The man's bald head shone in the dim light. His wife, dressed from head to toe in a black velvet pantsuit, had a clump of pearls around her neck and a silver bracelet stacked with charms on her wrist. Rylee offered them a friendly smile while piling nuts into a bowl.

It was almost 10:00 p.m. on a Friday. The subtle lighting in the bar area of the Promenade Steak House accentuated the muted colors of the liquor bottles on display. The bottles were translucent, ranging from small and round to tall and slender. Each one was dressed differently; some had dark wood-paneled labels with neat handwriting, while others sported clear glass, revealing the beverage's hue.

A man with reddish hair and brilliant green eyes dropped on the stool directly before her.

"Hey, Seth," she him greeted warmly, then asked, "what are you drinking tonight?" Rylee spoke loudly so he could hear her over the many conversations going on in the bar area.

"Whiskey sour," came the response. "I just left a party, and to be honest, I need a drink."

"How many did you have at the party?" Rylee asked.

"There wasn't any alcohol. That's why I came here."

She soaked in the laughter and the energy of the patrons as she served him quickly.

He took a sip, then said, "No one makes a whiskey sour the way you do, Rylee."

She grinned. "Thanks, Seth."

He was a regular and one of her favorite customers. He was always respectful and a great tipper. Seth's drinks were either a whiskey sour, a beer or a cognac on the rocks.

He handed her a twenty-dollar bill. "Keep the change."

She smiled and moved down the bar. Everyone looked successful in their expensive suits and business attire. She caught a glimpse of herself in the large mirror behind her. Rylee examined her reflection. She and her coworker were the only ones who looked *normal* in tuxedo shirts and black slacks. That was the idea. In a high-end restaurant such as this, the employees were not supposed to stand out—only the drinks and the food.

A server walked up and asked for a glass of the house red wine for a customer in the dining room.

Rylee accommodated her request, then placed a second mug of beer in front of her next patron. She'd never been a drinker, so it amazed Rylee how her customers were able to keep laughing and drinking for so many hours.

"Hey, gorgeous… Can I get a drink?"

The request jolted Rylee out of her thoughts. The voice had a mysterious quality to it. "Of course. What would you like?"

Rylee faced the man with dark eyes and black hair. She had never seen him here before tonight. New faces were not uncommon, but his intense gaze sent shivers up her arms. This time her intuition was on high alert.

He stared at her with an emotionless smirk. "I'll have a Jack Daniel's on the rocks."

She grabbed the bottle and poured a shot of the dark liquor into a glass filled with ice. Rylee placed it in front of him, then glanced up at the clock on the wall. Her shift was ending soon. She'd been at work since noon and looked forward to soaking in the tub when she got home. Her days were much more monotonous than they'd been fifteen months ago. Sometimes she missed her old life, but other days she was happy for the quiet.

"Where're you from?" the man asked.

Rylee gave him a polite smile, then, as casually as she could manage, she asked, "Why don't you start off by telling me your name?" He already knew hers because of her employee badge.

"Luis," he responded with a grin that was likely meant to dazzle her but failed.

She eyed him. Her guard was up, but Rylee kept her face friendly. "It's nice to meet you, Luis. I'm from Seattle. And you? What brings you to Racine?" The lie was becoming easier.

As Luis removed his gloves, Rylee noticed the old bruises on his knuckles. A shiver ran down her spine as she recognized the sinister energy that emanated from the man. Dressed in faded black jeans, a turtleneck and a leather jacket, he looked at her with a predatory gaze that made her feel exposed and vulnerable.

Luis's flat, hard eyes held her still as he spoke. "Chicago. I'm in town on business for a few days." He downed his drink in one gulp, never once breaking eye contact with her. "I'm an accountant."

Rylee's heart began to pound heavily in her chest. Pointing to his empty glass, she asked, "Would you like another one?" She hoped to end the conversation and get away from him as quickly as possible.

"No, I'm good." Luis pulled a ten out of his wallet and laid it on the counter. "The maître d' just signaled that my table's ready."

As he walked away, Rylee breathed a sigh of relief. It was only then that she realized how tightly she had been holding on to the edge of the bar.

"It was nice meeting you, *Rylee*," he called back over his shoulder.

She watched as he disappeared into the crowd, feeling like prey being stalked by a predator. Rylee tried to shake the uneasiness, but it wouldn't release its grip on her.

A young woman dressed in an identical uniform as Rylee walked behind the bar—this was her replacement. Rylee gave her a quick update before walking briskly to the staff room.

She snatched her puffy coat, scarf and gloves out of her locker, slipping them on quickly. She retrieved her leather backpack and the hat sticking out of it. She glanced uneasily over her shoulder as she clocked out. Normally, she ordered a meal to take home with her, but not tonight. Rylee couldn't wait to escape to the safety of her apartment.

She pushed back against the wave of apprehension swirling in her gut. Everyone believed that Rolanda Green was dead. There wasn't anyone looking for her. The hospital staff had all been instructed to report her death. Rylee tried to convince herself that she was overreacting.

Get a grip, Rylee. She placed the knit hat on her head. *Don't stop trusting your gut now.*

The eighteen-degree weather rudely slapped Rylee in the face when she exited the employees' door. In all this time, she still hadn't gotten used to the Racine weather, but she'd learned how to drive safely when it snowed.

Rylee always parked her Honda Accord in a well-lit area and away from other cars. Taser in hand, she surveyed her surroundings, then hurriedly made her way to her vehicle. She unlocked the driver-side door and climbed inside. She spared a glance at the ebony-colored car with the silver trim parked next to hers as she drove away.

Rylee's stomach felt like it was doing somersaults as she pulled onto the road. Her heart hammered against her chest as each second ticked by. Willing the car in front to speed up, her knuckles blanched with tension as she wrestled with the steering wheel. A chill raced down her spine as she glanced into her rearview mirror, afraid she wouldn't be alone. Since entering the witness protection program, Rylee had refused to become complacent. Letting her guard down could prove deadly. After trying to take down the notorious Mancuso cartel, she'd lost her partner and her life in LA. An image of the man responsible flashed in her mind. Calderon. A top lieutenant in the cartel. He was still out there, and she'd never lost her drive to expose him. Had he found her?

She glanced up at the rearview mirror again and noticed a dark vehicle two cars behind her. The stirrings of caution prickled at the back of her neck when it suddenly maneuvered around the other vehicles to get directly behind her. She recognized the car as the one that was parked beside hers earlier. The silver trim gleamed beneath the streetlights.

Rylee deliberately drove past her apartment building, hoping the driver would turn onto the upcoming street.

The car kept at a safe distance but continued to follow her.

She made a right turn two blocks from where she lived. Her heart rate picked up when the car following her did the same. The driver was definitely tailing her.

"Call Easton Bennett," she said clearly to voice command.

When her handler answered, Rylee stated, "I'm being followed. I recognized the car from the restaurant. It was parked right beside mine earlier."

"You know where to meet me?"

"I do," she responded. "I'll be there after I lose this person."

"I'm on my way," he said. "I'm about fifteen minutes out."

Rylee imposed an iron control on herself and sped up.

The car behind her immediately gained speed to keep up with her.

Rylee clenched her jaw, reached inside her glove compartment and pulled out a gun. When the vehicle was beside her, she glanced over and saw it was Luis, the man from the restaurant.

Grinning, he gestured for her to pull over.

When Rylee showed no signs of doing what he wanted, his grin became more menacing.

She met his sinister eyes without flinching. Rylee drew a deep breath, forbade herself to tremble and pressed down on the gas pedal, increasing her speed.

She ran a red light.

Luis followed and was T-boned by a car, the initial impact between the two vehicles creating a loud, sharp crash.

"Yessss…" Rylee didn't feel an ounce of regret for cheering on the person who'd hit Luis. She pulled over. Shattered glass and remnants from the vehicle were sprinkled in the street. She prayed his car was rendered completely useless. At least the accident would help widen the distance between them. She put the car in Drive and took off.

Rylee jumped on the highway for four miles, then took the first exit ramp, using a side road to get to the designated meeting spot, an abandoned warehouse. She used a remote

Easton had given her to enter the building, closing the door behind her.

She turned the car around so that she faced the entrance, then turned off her lights. She pulled out a pair of jeans from her backpack and changed into them, then exchanged the white tuxedo shirt for a black sweater. She had to be ready for anything.

Gun in hand, she waited in her car. There was no doubt in her mind who'd sent Luis.

What puzzled her most was how that man could've found her. She'd done everything by the book and had given up everything so that no one ever would…

Easton arrived a few minutes later.

She got out of the car. "*What happened?* Who blew my cover, because I sure didn't. Everyone is supposed to believe I died along with my partner. This man walked right up to the bar and started a conversation with me. He said his name was Luis."

Easton approached, hands in his pockets. "Are you sure he wasn't some dude just trying to get to know you? You're a very attractive woman, Rylee."

"Maybe it was the bruises on his knuckles that make me seriously doubt he wanted me to pull over just to talk." Rylee was furious. "How did they find me?"

"This is a huge problem if my office has suddenly sprung a leak," he responded.

She knew it wasn't Easton's fault, but she'd never felt so vulnerable as she did now, and Rylee didn't like the feeling. "Let's go with the assumption that Calderon sent someone after me until you find out differently. Did you call anyone after you talked to me?"

Easton shook his head. "No, I came straight here. Right

now, I don't know who I can trust in the agency, so we're on our own."

"How could that have happened?"

"I don't know," he said, "but I'm gonna find out. We've never had anything like this happen here."

"And what about this place? Does anyone know about it? How can you be sure that it's safe?" Rylee asked. Once she was someplace safe—they could try to figure out the leak.

"It's safe. My uncle owns this building." Pointing to a black SUV with tinted windows parked a few feet away, Easton stated, "We're leaving in that."

Rylee always kept a small suitcase in her car in case this moment ever arrived. She grabbed it along with her backpack, then strode over to the SUV and climbed inside.

She swallowed hard as shivers snaked down her arms. "I could tell there was something off about that man. I can't explain it, but the moment he looked at me—it was like he knew who I was. His eyes…" Rylee couldn't finish the thought. She ran trembling fingers through her shoulder-length hair as her steady resolve began to wilt. "I've always been extremely careful. I never once broke protocol."

"I'm gonna find the leak. In the meantime, we'll put you somewhere safe."

"We never saw this guy coming, Easton," she uttered with a slight edge of defiance. "I'm telling you now. I won't make the mistake of foolishly believing that I'm totally safe again. I could've just taken my chances at home instead of freezing here in Racine."

"I know what you're thinking… Rylee, you can't go back to Los Angeles. It's really not safe for you there."

Staring out the window, she responded, "Apparently, it's no longer safe for me to stay dead, either."

EASTON HAD RYLEE toss her phone out of the window as they left Racine.

"I'll get you a new one," he told her.

He seemed to be driving around in circles to ensure they weren't being followed. He drove to a secluded area in Milwaukee. He turned off the lights, pulled off the road and parked at a distance, scanning what he could see of the property.

Rylee surveyed the area as well. Shadows transformed from one shape to another as beams of moonlight danced from tree to tree. Her heart pounded wildly as she searched and listened. A physical barrier and camera surveillance enclosed the safe house where they would spend the next few days.

Under normal circumstances, Easton and another marshal would provide twenty-four-hour protection whenever a witness was in a high-threat condition, but Rylee knew he thought it best to work alone at this moment. She agreed.

"Everything looks exactly as it should." Easton started the ignition and drove the rest of the way.

They entered the dark house through the garage.

Inside was a network of anti-intrusion systems and closed-circuit cameras that monitored the grounds, corridors and doors. This house differed greatly from the safe site she'd stayed in during her orientation in Washington, DC. That facility consisted of a one-bedroom suite with an exterior courtyard surrounded by high concrete walls, from which Rylee could hear other witnesses but had no idea who they were or what they looked like. She was never allowed to have physical contact with any of them and couldn't leave her living quarters unescorted.

During that time, the marshals had provided groceries and any other items she required, including Rylee's pain medication during her recovery. They also supplied her with books, maps and newspapers to familiarize her with Racine. She had been given a choice as to where she wanted to live and chose Wisconsin over Iowa. She also had to study similar information to support her cover story—information on Seattle—the city she would tell others she was from.

Racine had finally started to feel like a place she could call home. She'd made a couple of wonderful friends at work and did normal things like going to movies, festivals and a couple of parties. She had no social media presence and wouldn't let anyone snap photos of her. She explained it away by telling her friends that some guy had stalked her.

"I can't believe we have to do this all over again," Rylee uttered, dropping her luggage on the floor in the living room. "If there's a leak, I'll never be safe. All my information needs to be scrubbed from your files. I can't stay in WITSEC."

Easton picked up his phone.

"Who are you calling?" she asked.

"A friend of mine. Don't worry," he responded. "He's no longer with the agency. I trust this man with my life, so I will have him meet us here. Then we'll decide our next move." He went into one of the rooms to talk to his friend.

Easton returned a few minutes later, saying, "I need to show you the basement. There's a panic room down there."

"Do you think we'll have to use it?" Rylee questioned.

"Nope, but I want you to know what to do if necessary."

Once down there, Easton pointed toward a large clock on a granite-covered wall. "There's a camera hidden in it. From inside the room, you can see what's going on down here only. The guy who designed the room didn't want anyone to spot any unusual wiring—that's why he didn't connect any of the cameras upstairs to here."

He led her over to the wall and showed her how to open

the hidden door. "There is a multipoint locking system installed."

Inside, Rylee glanced around at the rustic design. She eyed the built-in bunk beds that extended beyond one wall. A plush sectional sofa and ottoman were in the center of the room. There was a TV, a compact refrigerator and a microwave. "This is some panic room."

"The door is bulletproof, and the walls are reinforced. You'll be safe in here. There's snacks in the pantry over there. Microwave meals in the fridge along with bottled water."

"Well, it's not like we'll be needing to stay in here," Rylee responded.

"Right, but I wanted you to know about it," Easton stated. "Better to know and not need it than not know."

Although he was trying hard not to show it, she could tell he was just as troubled as she was.

They returned to the main level. Rylee planted herself in the living room and pulled the nine-millimeter Glock out of her backpack.

Easton's eyes widened in surprise. "Where on earth did you get that?"

"I bought it from a guy I met at the restaurant," she responded nonchalantly. "He comes to the bar every time he's in town. He mentioned one evening that he had one to sell, so I bought it." She didn't mention that she'd bought a second one from him as well.

"I shouldn't have to tell you how risky—"

"I have to protect myself, Easton. Look, I'm not some criminal. I have a permit for it."

She pointed to the chessboard. "Wanna play?" The discussion had come to an end as far as Rylee was concerned. There was no way she'd be without weapons to protect herself. She'd trusted her partner, Stuart, with her entire being and almost lost her life. She trusted Easton to protect her, and now they were on the run. Armed with a Taser, her Glock and the other gun in her backpack, Rylee felt better prepared to defend herself should it come to that.

"Sure," Easton responded. "When did you learn to play?"

"Promenade hosts a chess tournament every year. I know how much you love it, so I thought I'd learn. I must warn you, though—I learned the game from one of the best."

Her handler offered one of his rare smiles. "Sounds like you'll be a challenge. I've been playing this game since I was in high school. I've even won a few championships myself."

Shrugging, Rylee chuckled. "Those days may be over. I'm just saying…"

After she beat him, Easton yawned and stretched. "I guess I was more exhausted than I thought. I normally beat the mess out of my opponents."

"Uh-huh…"

He settled back on the couch. "You go and try to get some sleep."

Rylee strode to the bedroom closest to the entrance. She made herself comfortable in the middle of the queen-size bed, pulled out her iPad and began reading.

Within minutes, unable to fully concentrate on the novel, Rylee gave up. She lay back against the pillows, willing her body to relax as she contemplated her future fully.

During the investigation, after she and Stuart were shot, fentanyl was found in her partner's house and two million dollars in his bank account linking him to the Mancuso cartel. Although Stuart and his wife had separated shortly before his death, Rylee's heart hurt for Elena and the children. She regretted not being able to personally offer her condolences or assurances that Stuart remained an agent with integrity and honor until the end of his watch. She'd never believed he was involved with the cartel.

Rylee was able to place a key member of the Mancuso cartel at the shooting, which was why she was placed in WITSEC. She missed her mother, who still lived in LA, every day.

Now that the cartel knew where she was, the bright side of her current dilemma was that she could finally go home.

She wanted to reach out to her department head at Homeland Security but decided to hold off for now. Rylee was steadfast in her belief that Stuart wasn't a drug trafficker. She wanted to clear her partner's name for his family. He was a good man—a shining example in all walks of life. There was no way he'd be involved in trafficking fentanyl. His mother had died of a heroin overdose when Stuart was fifteen. He hated drugs with a passion and fought diligently to get them off the streets. Rylee had joined Homeland Security for a similar reason—her younger brother had had a cocaine addiction. She'd left the marines after six years to help her mother with him. Unfortunately, he'd died two months later. That was when she'd applied to join Homeland Security Investigations.

Rylee lay back against the pillows, pushing the painful memories away. When she finally drifted off to sleep, the familiar dream returned—the one where she and Stuart found themselves face-to-face with a group of armed men, and one of them was Calderon.

"You don't want to do this. We're not alone," Stuart bluffed. "This place is surrounded."

Rylee knew the truth. There was no one coming to their aid. No one knew they'd come to the waterfront that day.

Before Stuart was shot, she'd heard him utter, "This was a setup."

Just as the shooter fired at her, Rylee was snatched awake by Easton.

"Get up," he urged. "We got visitors. Three men with guns."

Rylee quickly slid out of bed and grabbed her Glock. She picked up her backpack to retrieve extra ammunition.

"What are you doing?" Easton asked.

"We're shooting our way out, right?" She found a perverse pleasure in the challenge of taking on the people sent to kill her. "I'm locked and loaded."

"Look, there's no time for this. Take your stuff. Leave no evidence that you were ever here. Move quickly and get to the panic room."

She paused long enough to ask, "What about you?"

"I'm staying out here. Now *go*...and stay there until I come for you. *Do not come out.* You remember the safe word?"

"Yes..."

"Go," Easton commanded.

Rylee did as he instructed. She grabbed her backpack and suitcase then rushed to the basement.

Once there, she sat down on the sofa to wait.

For what, she had no idea.

The only question on her mind was, how did they find her so quickly?

Chapter Two

Kaleb Stone killed the engine of his truck and got out. He eyed the ground, noting the two sets of tire tracks. He went back to his vehicle and climbed inside, then waited for the gate in front of the safe house to swing open so he could enter.

Unholstering his weapon, he stayed low as he stealthily approached the cabin-style house from the north. Kaleb closed in on the front door, where he was supposed to meet Easton. His friend had called him and asked for his assistance with a witness. Easton had sounded worried on the phone, which prompted Kaleb to come as soon as he could.

He tested the handle, and the door swung open.

This wasn't a good sign.

A dead man lay in the middle of the living room floor.

Definitely not a good sign.

His own breathing cut through the silence as Kaleb ventured inside, his gun raised at shoulder level, ready to fire. Faint hints of moonlight penetrated through the windows, casting shadows throughout the space. He moved deeper into the house, walking stealthily through the living and kitchen area.

Kaleb took another step.

The crunching of glass filled his ears as he walked over the shards. He lifted his foot, recognizing the phone that belonged to Easton. A thread of warning tickled the back of his neck as Kaleb imagined what had taken place before his arrival.

Weapon aimed, Kaleb made his way to the first bedroom at the front of the house. Looking down, he eyed the dark spots that led the way to the door.

His stomach clenched as he entered the room, stumbling over another body. Kaleb bent down and sighed in relief when the dead man wasn't Easton. He stepped farther into the room...and found his friend. Blood seeped from a bullet wound to his head and one to his chest.

His heart in his throat, Kaleb checked for a pulse, although he already knew he wouldn't find one. "Sorry I couldn't get here sooner, old friend..." A wave of sadness washed over him as he stood up. Easton had been his mentor when Kaleb was a recruit with the US marshals' agency. He was determined to find out who did this to his friend.

He strode out of the room with purpose, searched the other two bedrooms and found them empty. He knew there was only one other place to check. Heading down to the basement, he hoped to find what he was looking for.

An hour had passed from the time Easton sent her down to the basement.

Rylee was antsy. Fear and anger knotted inside her as she tried to stay optimistic. Easton should've come for her by now.

Relax...he's probably ensuring everything's safe before he comes to get me. Another thought entered her mind. *What if they're torturing him—or worse?*

It was impossible to steady her erratic pulse, so she paced while trying to devise a backup plan. She had to consider all avenues. Easton had told her there were three men with guns—he was only one man. She and Easton could've taken them down between the two of them.

The room was soundproof, so she couldn't hear anything. At least with the camera embedded in the clock, she would see them coming if they discovered the panic room somehow.

Rylee glimpsed movement and walked over to the monitor, catching sight of someone dressed in a dark hoodie and sweatpants. She could tell by his build and the way he walked that it wasn't Easton.

He said nobody knew about this room.

Not only did the stranger know it was there—he also knew the code.

Panic like she'd never known welled in her throat. Rylee pulled her gun and aimed it at the entrance.

The door slid open, revealing a man she had never seen before. He was tall like Easton, but more on the athletic side. He slowly removed his hood to reveal his warm caramel complexion and gray eyes.

"Whoa…" he uttered, holding his hands up in the air.

"If you take one more step, I'll put a bullet between your eyes," Rylee stated, her tone firm.

"I believe you," he responded. "I'm a friend of Easton's. Kaleb Stone is my name. He called me because he wanted my help."

"What's the safe word?" she asked. The muscles in the back of her legs braced instinctively, waiting for whatever came next. "You have one chance to get it right. *I mean it.*"

"Maximum risk."

Rylee dropped her arm by her side but didn't holster her gun. The fluorescent lighting overhead cast shadows along the stranger's angled jawline as he stepped into the space, highlighting the perfect curve of his mouth. "Where's Easton?"

He seemed to hesitate. "I found him in a bedroom... fatally shot," he answered thickly.

Tears burned in her eyes, blurring her vision. Another good man gone. She shook her head regretfully, then swiped at her eyes. Easton was not only her handler, but he was also a friend. He'd been the only person Rylee could truly be herself with for the past fifteen months. She struggled to contain her anger and grief. Now was not the time to fall apart.

"I'm here to make sure you stay safe," Kaleb stated. "I promised Easton."

"My hero," Rylee muttered. "Easton should've told you I'm more than capable of taking care of myself. He may have trusted you, but I don't know you well enough to say I feel the same way."

"Understood."

Vivid gray eyes fastened on her, and suddenly Rylee felt as if Kaleb Stone could see straight through her. She wondered if he could sense her fear of never seeing her mother again. Or her frustration in not being able to prove Stuart's innocence and having to give up her freedom. Rylee didn't intend to spend the rest of her life in hiding. She was simply biding her time.

"You may not trust me, but right now I'm the only person on your side." Kaleb paused a moment before adding, "We need to get out of here."

He was right, although Rylee hated to admit it. Right now, this stranger was her only way of escape.

KALEB KEPT HIS eyes on the road ahead, not on Rylee in the back seat. She hadn't said a word since they'd left the safe house. He tried but couldn't ignore the fact she'd been chewing on her bottom lip since she'd gotten in the truck. Or the fact that she kept her gun in her right hand.

Whenever they neared a traffic light, she bent down to avoid any traffic cams.

Oncoming headlights reflected off the windshield as Kaleb took the shortest route out of Milwaukee to Mukwonago.

"We can go our separate ways once I have a solid plan," Rylee blurted suddenly.

"That's not happening," he responded.

"Excuse me?"

Kaleb glanced at her in the rearview. "Easton asked for my help, and even though he's gone, I'm a man of my word. Rylee, as long as you listen to me and do what I tell you to do, I'll keep you safe."

"I'm not going back into WITSEC."

"I'm not a US marshal anymore," Kaleb responded. "I own a private security firm."

He drove his truck down a long alley behind a mechanic's shop in Mukwonago. Motion-sensor lights lit up their approach, highlighting the rich black color of her hair.

Kaleb parked in front of an old body shop. He studied the dilapidated-looking shop with a roll-up door to the garage for signs of movement. "We're here."

Rylee eyed the dust-caked windows with disdain. "You and Easton really have a thing for old buildings. I thought you were taking me to another safe house."

"Anything can be used for a safe house," Kaleb responded. "Best to go unnoticed. My brother and I converted this place last year in case Easton needed a safe place. Completely off the grid." He reached into the back seat for a black overnight bag he kept on hand. He felt a rush of heat the moment his arm brushed against hers.

Kaleb gripped the bag's handle tighter than necessary to counter the effect. She'd awarded him one brief smile, which remained vivid in his mind as he climbed out of the truck.

The moment he'd opened the door to the panic room and laid eyes on Rylee, an undeniable electricity had sizzled through his entire body. He chided himself for allowing his mind to be consumed with thoughts of her. Kaleb needed to focus on keeping her alive.

Losing a witness he was supposed to protect was the reason he was no longer a deputy marshal.

He walked briskly to the passenger side to relieve Rylee of her suitcase, then headed to the garage. Kaleb entered a four-digit code to unlock the front door. "We're only staying here for a day or so."

"If this place is so safe, why are we moving again?" Rylee asked. "What aren't you telling me?"

"Nobody knows about this place. I just like to keep moving when I'm protecting someone. You can relax."

"I'm not so sure about people not knowing about it. Easton said no one knew about the other place. Turns out, he was wrong."

Hinges screamed in protest from the weight of the heavy steel door as Kaleb led her inside. He hit the lights.

Kaleb hadn't been back here since Nate completed the renovations. The space was much larger than he remembered. He navigated to the surveillance room to check the monitors. Several other rooms were located down a wide hallway.

He glanced over at Rylee. "You can go to the first bedroom on the left to freshen up if you'd like."

She glanced at Kaleb. "Thank you."

He could tell she didn't trust him yet…but trusting him was her only option.

ONCE IN THE BEDROOM, Rylee removed her shirt and washed off. She eyed her reflection, noting the scars left from the bullet wound to her torso and the one that had grazed the left side of her head. The face of the man who'd given the order appeared in her mind.

Calderon.

She hungered to take him down, but that alone wouldn't quell her thirst for revenge. Life in prison wasn't enough, and death was too easy for a man as ruthless as Calderon. She took some satisfaction that her survival must torture his thoughts. If he knew she was alive, then he knew she could testify against him. Calderon's luck would eventually run out, and he'd get what he deserved—Rylee hoped sooner rather than later.

When she returned to the living room, Kaleb strode out of the kitchen with some takeout menus. "These restaurants are open twenty-four hours. I thought you might be hungry, so what would you like to eat?"

"Pizza," Rylee responded. "Veggie."

"Great. The restaurant is just a block away. I'll order and pick it up."

She sat down on the red leather couch while he placed their order, then Kaleb sat down in one of the matching accent chairs. It was hard to believe that only four hours had passed since she'd left her job. In that time, Rylee had had to leave one safe house for another, Easton had been murdered and now she was under the protection of a stranger.

"It should be ready in twenty minutes," Kaleb stated while they waited. He wanted her to feel comfortable, so he tried to find some common ground between them. "Nice Glock, by the way. Small enough to carry concealed and large enough to hit your target."

She nodded. "I wanted this one because it takes ten-, fifteen-, seventeen- and thirty-three-round magazines— plenty of options if I have to deal with a threat," Rylee said.

He studied her. "If I had to guess, I'd say you are ex-military…even law enforcement. It's obvious you know your way around a gun, and I haven't seen you flinch once even with everything that's happened."

"Both," she responded and rolled up her sleeve to show a tattoo of the marines insignia.

"Semper Fi…" Kaleb revealed a similar tattoo on his chest. "First of the First Battalion."

She smiled. "I was with the Second Reconnaissance Battalion."

"You were stationed at Camp Lejeune."

She nodded. "Yeah."

"You didn't want to make it a career?" Kaleb asked.

"I got out because my family needed me more."

She didn't explain, and he was curious to learn more about her but checked his watch. "It's time for me to pick up the pizza. I won't be gone long."

She broke into a smile. "I'll be right here when you get back."

Kaleb eyed her.

"Really… I'm not going anywhere. I'm hungry, so I'll hang around long enough to eat. After that, I'm not making any promises."

He nodded and walked out to his truck. *How am I supposed to keep Rylee safe if she is so determined to take off on her own?*

Kaleb returned with the food to find her sitting on the sofa, remote in hand, surfing television channels.

"You're still here," he said, half teasing.

"I told you I'd stay around long enough to eat," Rylee responded. There was a glint of humor in her eyes.

He smiled. "Yes, you did."

They sat down at the large table in the dining room, and Kaleb handed her a paper plate.

"Thank you." She retrieved a slice of pizza. "So, you own a private security firm."

"I do. My brother is my partner."

"You must have some interesting clients," she said with a glint of wonder.

"I guess you can say that." Kaleb sat back in his chair, watching her. "You never told me what agency you worked with."

"Homeland Security," Rylee stated.

"How did you end up in WITSEC?" he asked.

"My partner and I went to check out a lead he'd received on a shipment of fentanyl and other drugs at Cabrillo Beach, and we were ambushed. They killed him, and they thought they'd killed me, too. But somehow, they found out that I'm still alive."

That surprised him… "You were investigating the Mancuso cartel? Easton didn't tell me anything other than he needed my help."

She nodded. "Not really. It wasn't our case—that's the thing. For some reason, my partner got a tip, and we checked things out. I didn't question him—I trusted Stuart." Rylee picked a single mushroom off her slice, sticking it into her mouth.

"How long have you known Easton?" she asked after sipping her drink.

"Easton was my mentor for eight years. I left the agency three years ago, but Easton and I remained friends." Kaleb opened a can of soda and took a long drink.

"He wasn't just my handler—he was also my friend. I really liked him."

"He was one of the good guys," he responded. "His daughter, Nova, is following in his footsteps. She's a deputy marshal." An image of a slender biracial woman flashed in his mind. She'd be devastated by her father's passing.

"Easton showed me a photograph of her once," Rylee said quietly. "He was very proud of her."

Kaleb nodded in agreement. "He was against her joining the agency initially, but Nova wore him down. Once he accepted it and watched how well she handled herself—Easton gave her his full support."

"Do you miss it? Working as a marshal?" Rylee finished off her slice, then reached for another.

"Not really," Kaleb responded with a shrug.

"What type of clients do you normally take on?"

"High-profile," he answered. "Like you. Also celebrities…"

Settling back in her seat, Rylee said, "I don't consider myself high-profile. I did everything I could to blend into the framework of Racine. I was settling into my new life and now, I'm a moving target."

"Not for long. I'll get you somewhere safe."

Settling back in her chair, Rylee said, "Easton and I believe there's a leak in the marshals' office."

"I know. That's why he called me in to ensure you stay alive."

"I need to go back to California, Kaleb. I can get my job with Homeland Security back and—"

"You're a key witness to murder and attempted murder, Rylee," he cut her off. "It's not safe for you outside of WITSEC."

She gave a nod. "I saw Calderon that night Stuart and I were ambushed. I can place him there. Right now, his freedom depends on my staying dead."

"He's been on the move for years to avoid being apprehended."

Rylee shrugged in nonchalance. "He's going to make a mistake eventually."

"Calderon is a dangerous man," Kaleb stated.

"I'm fighting to stay alive. I'd say that makes me dangerous as well."

He chuckled. "Remind me never to get on your bad side."

She laughed, looking more relaxed, then pushed her plate away. "I've just had two slices of pizza...probably not the healthiest of choices, but it was so worth it."

"After everything that's happened, I'm glad you can eat something."

"I'm a foodie." She shrugged. "Eating is never a problem for me."

"Did you happen to get a good look at the men who came to the house?" he asked. Kaleb had wanted to ask her earlier but didn't want to overwhelm her. He needed her to trust him.

"No. Everything happened so fast," Rylee responded. "What about the security camera? Maybe you can look at the video of that night."

"I'll have my brother check it out."

"I'd like to see the footage as well," she said. "I want to see the faces of the people who came to kill me."

Chapter Three

Rylee downed the last of her bottled water while Kaleb finished off his second slice of pizza. "It's no longer safe for me to stay in Wisconsin," she said with fearful clarity. "I might as well go back to LA. My mother's there, and I want to see her. I've been away for fifteen months. I want to go *home*. But before I can see her, I have to find the people responsible for Stuart's death and for trying to kill me."

"I have to tell you, I think it's an wild idea," he responded.

She lifted her chin in defiance. "And I disagree."

"Rylee, you're in *real* danger. The Mancuso family controls one of the largest drug territories in the country. You're a serious threat to that organization."

"I'm sure they're doing some reorganizing right now. Raul Mancuso was murdered six months after I went into WITSEC. With any luck, Calderon will be behind bars soon. I read that four of his trucks were confiscated in an Arizona raid last month. He took a huge hit there. There's already been a couple of cartel wars..." Rylee kept current on news concerning the Mancuso cartel and silently counted every arrest made and quantity of drugs confiscated as a small victory.

"Doesn't matter," Kaleb stated. "Calderon's not the only person you have to worry about. The other is Raul's widow."

Rylee's eyebrows rose in surprise. "Poppy Mancuso?" She broke into a short laugh. "She's nothing more than arm candy."

"Word on the street is that she oversees all her late husband's territories. Also, she's more ruthless than Raul. Poppy is suspected of killing her former lover. A month after his death, she married Raul, his boss. And now he's dead, too…"

Over the years, Poppy, a former model, had been painted as a spoiled woman who loved shopping, traveling and fine dining. But the only articles Rylee had come across mentioning Poppy lately spoke of how she had a heart for children and had established several orphanages in Mexico and South America.

"I'm assuming this is just a theory—none of it has been proven," Rylee stated. "I know she spends most of her time in Ecuador… She's untouchable when she's there."

He nodded. "Poppy comes to the States from time to time, but it's never for a long period."

"How do you know so much about the cartel?" Rylee asked.

"I've had some dealings with them in the past. I worked with Easton before opening my own business."

She nodded. "Is there any surveillance on this woman?"

"Some, but nothing incriminating as far as I know," Kaleb responded. "Some people believe that Calderon has taken control, but I'm not buying it. From what I've heard…he reports to Poppy."

Rylee searched her memory. When she was at HSI, Poppy's name hadn't come up much, except that she was married to Raul. "I can't see Calderon being led around by a female. He doesn't seem the type. Maybe Calderon's her lover, but I'm betting he's in charge. Maybe she is exactly what she seems—a woman of leisure. I do believe that he would've betrayed Raul at some point. Maybe Calderon is the person who murdered him."

"I don't know about that. The two men were close friends, but regardless of who's in charge, Rylee, you can't take on this cartel alone."

"Are you volunteering your help?"

"I'll do everything I can to keep you safe."

"I'm not afraid of Poppy Mancuso or Calderon."

"That's what bothers me," Kaleb said. "They *should* scare you."

She gave him a pointed look. "You seem to know a lot about the Mancuso cartel."

"A few years ago, I worked with a wealthy family to get their son out of the cartel. He was a college student who got caught up. He was a mule, but one night his car was stolen. When it was recovered, the eighty kilograms of cocaine hidden in a secret compartment had gone missing. They were going to kill him. We gave him and his parents new identities and a new life."

"I suppose their deaths were faked so the cartel wouldn't keep looking for them," Rylee surmised.

"We didn't fake their deaths. My brother and I just made sure their identities could never be discovered. They are safe in another country."

"You mentioned your brother…he designed the panic room…is he an architect?"

Kaleb nodded. "He was also military intelligence and knows his way around a computer."

"You mean he's a hacker." Rylee smiled.

Kaleb laughed. The deep sound sent tremors shooting through her. In this moment, life felt normal. She was a woman enjoying a conversation with a man.

A very handsome man—although there was no room for romance in her life at the moment.

"Can you get me information on Poppy Mancuso?" she asked.

He nodded. "I can do that right now. You need to know who you're trying to go up against."

Rylee shivered a little from the drop in temperature. She couldn't wait to escape the Wisconsin weather. She would miss the cheese curds and the fish boils that were popular among the locals, but they were worth giving up in favor of palm trees and sunshine.

She was willing to give up just about anything to put Calderon behind bars.

AFTER AN HOUR on the computer, Kaleb walked out of the office and handed Rylee a folder. "Here is all the information I could gather on Poppy. She has a colorful history."

She quickly reviewed the file. "You're right about that. Working at Homeland Security, we figured Calderon would take over. He was Raul's right hand for years."

"He's still the top soldier in the organization and the primary threat. But you need to know all the players."

According to the information Kaleb had been able to pull together, Poppy Moreno Mancuso was no stranger to the workings of the cartel. Authorities believed that she possessed full knowledge of her husband's drug trafficking business, which included controlling smuggling routes into California, Arizona and Texas.

Rylee laid the folder on the sofa beside her. "If we can believe this stuff, Poppy's not a minimal participant in this organization. This woman knows where all the bodies are buried. The drug routes, sources of supply for fentanyl, Xanax and cocaine as well as corrupt public officials..."

She picked up the folder and scanned the documents once more. "She's suspected of being involved with Raul's tunnel escape from a prison in Mexico ten years ago. Poppy can do a lot of damage to the cartel."

"She could, but don't count on her talking," Kaleb said.

"Probably not. But if this information is true about her being a philanthropist—do you actually believe this woman is willing to risk spending the rest of her life in prison?"

He met her gaze. "That's the thing…you'll have to catch her first. That woman knows how to slip in and out of this country—she's a chameleon."

"Once Calderon goes down, we might have a chance at successfully dismantling a large chunk of the operation."

She could tell Kaleb thought it was wishful thinking on Rylee's part.

"I'm going to do something to my hair and then take a shower," Rylee announced. It was almost 4:00 a.m., but she wasn't sleepy.

"Do you need anything?"

She rose. "Nope. I saw a pair of scissors in the bedroom, so I have everything I need."

He wore a look of confusion. "Scissors?"

"I'm switching up my look by cutting my hair. That way I can move around more freely."

He eyed her skeptically. "You're really about to cut your hair?"

"Yes. It'll grow back," Rylee said as she made her way down the hall.

In the bedroom was a twin bed and a dresser. Rylee walked into the bathroom and stared at her reflection in the mirror. She pulled her shoulder-length hair out of its ponytail holder.

She took the scissors and quickly began cutting before she changed her mind. They'd found her twice now—she'd do anything she could to throw them off her tail.

Rylee showered, then slipped into a pair of baggy blue

jeans, an oversize men's Lakers basketball jersey, a cap and dark sunglasses. She'd purchased the clothes months ago just in case her cover was blown. Back then, she'd had no idea that she'd ever need to actually wear the outfit, but once they arrived in Los Angeles, Rylee felt this would allow her to move around the city without detection.

She stared at her reflection again; her hair was still wet from her shower and lay in tiny curls. Rylee instantly regretted that she hadn't thought to purchase a couple of wigs instead of chopping off her long locks.

Too late now.

She gulped hard, hot tears slipping down her cheeks.

Rylee put the toilet seat down and sat, her hands to her face. Her clamped lips imprisoned a sob. Her life was once again turned upside down. She'd hoped for months that Calderon would be arrested. Three years ago, a federal indictment was issued, accusing him of conspiring to send large amounts of drugs into the US and using firearms during the commission of drug-trafficking crimes. However, authorities had been unsuccessful in apprehending him.

I want my life back.

Rylee understood the reality of her situation. She knew it wouldn't be easy to take down Calderon and completely dismantle a cartel such as the Mancuso organization, but it wasn't entirely impossible. However, it wasn't something she could do alone.

Rylee eased out of the bathroom and walked to the front of the house. She peeked into the living room. Kaleb was lying on the sofa. She couldn't tell if he was watching television or sleeping.

She tiptoed back to the bedroom and lay down.

I need to try and get some sleep. It's been a long night.

Chapter Four

Kaleb released a sigh of relief when Rylee returned to the bedroom, closing the door behind her. He was tired and needed to catch up on some much-needed sleep. He hoped and prayed she'd sleep for a few hours—Kaleb was sure she had to be just as exhausted as he was. But then, he'd been up for almost twenty-four hours now.

He got up and rechecked the security cameras before returning to the couch. There were two other bedrooms, but Kaleb preferred sleeping in the central area, which provided him the greatest advantage against intruders.

Stretching out, he made himself comfortable.

He woke up four hours later.

Kaleb called the local police department in Milwaukee instead of the US marshals' agency, because, like Easton, he didn't know whom to trust. The police would investigate the shooting at the safe house and contact the marshals. He thought it wise to keep Rylee's whereabouts a secret from everybody until they could find out more about the leak in the marshals.

A smile tugged at his lips as he recalled their initial meeting when the door opened to the panic room. Rylee wasn't bluffing. He did not doubt that she would've put a bullet between his eyes without so much as a blink. Kaleb liked her spirit.

He quietly made his way to her bedroom, noting that the door wasn't closed all the way. Kaleb peeked inside.

Rylee was curled in a fetal position and sleeping soundly.

He returned to the office to check the surveillance cameras, then navigated back to the couch and lay back down.

When he opened his eyes again, it was shortly after noon. Kaleb didn't hear movement coming from the bedroom and assumed Rylee must still be sleeping. He decided not to disturb her.

"What do you think?" Rylee asked when she paraded out of the bedroom later that afternoon in a basketball jersey and jeans. She did a slow turn in the center of the living room. She slipped on a pair of sunglasses, then she tried walking with a more manly vibe.

Kaleb bit back his amusement, but he couldn't deny that changing her appearance might aid in keeping Rylee safe. The choppy haircut did nothing to conceal her beauty. If her intent was to make herself look like a man, it wasn't working for him, but Kaleb decided not to tell her this. "It could work. But you'll need a different coat—something more masculine."

"You're right. I didn't think about that, but then again...I figured I had more time to formulate my disguise."

"Did you manage to get some sleep?" he asked.

"I did. I woke up late. Then I stayed in bed for another thirty minutes. How about you?"

"I was up earlier for a little while," Kaleb responded. "I went back down."

"So, what's the plan? How are you going to get me back to Los Angeles?"

"Why don't we figure out what we want to eat first?" Kaleb suggested.

"Works for me," Rylee replied with a slight shrug. "I'm

hungry. Can you order me a salad, with shrimp or black-ened salmon?"

He was ninety-nine percent sure they hadn't been followed to the safe house. Still, Kaleb decided it was best they leave later this evening. Kaleb sent a quick text to his brother before going to pick up the food.

Rylee was already seated in the dining room when he returned. He laid the food out and sat down to eat.

"This looks delicious." She stabbed a fork into a grilled shrimp and a piece of lettuce, then stuck it in her mouth. "This is good."

Kaleb watched Rylee's eyes close as she appeared to savor the flavors of her meal.

"I'm glad you're enjoying it."

She pointed to his club sandwich. "Have you ever eaten at this place before?"

"A few times."

"There's one in Racine," Rylee said. "I never tried it, though. I mainly stuck to the restaurants in my neighborhood. I rarely ventured out unless I was going to Milwaukee with my friends."

"It's good you were cautious."

They continued to make small talk as they ate.

After they finished, Kaleb said, "I need to make a few phone calls. I shouldn't be too long."

Rylee glanced over at him. "I don't recall if I've said thanks for what you did. I appreciate you coming to my aid."

Kaleb smiled. "It's my pleasure."

"Just know that I'm not some damsel in distress," Rylee stated. "If Easton hadn't sent me to the panic room, we probably could've taken all of them out."

A sense of guilt and sorrow hung heavily in the air.

"Easton wasn't willing to risk your life."

"There's a chance he would still be alive if he'd let me help, or if he'd just come to the panic room with me."

"Rylee, his death isn't on you. I hope you know that."

He glimpsed a glimmer of sadness in her eyes before it faded away. Kaleb understood what she was feeling in that moment. He'd felt that same way right before he left the marshals' service…weighed down by the guilt of having lost a witness.

THROUGHOUT THE DAY, Rylee noticed Kaleb kept glancing out the window, as if he was looking for someone.

She regarded him with somber curiosity. "Expecting company?"

"Yeah," he responded. "My brother, Nate, is on the way to pick us up. He should be here in about an hour."

"Why does he need to pick us up? Your car is in the garage." She placed her backpack in her lap.

"You can relax, Rylee," Kaleb said. "I could've driven straight to Whitefish Bay, but I wanted to be absolutely sure that we weren't being followed. I've found that it's good to change vehicles every now and then."

"Why don't we just leave Wisconsin altogether?" she asked. "Especially since this is where they're looking for me."

"I'm sure they're expecting you to head back to California, which is why you have to be patient. It's best to have a plan before we do that. We also need to get new identification for you…"

"I *do* have a plan, Kaleb," Rylee interjected. "I intend on making sure Calderon pays for Stuart's death and trying to make it look as if he was corrupt. I want to clear Stuart's name for his family." Calderon was present when she and her partner were ambushed and had ordered the hits. "He also needs to pay for shooting me and killing Easton. I'm sure he's the one who sent Luis. What I can't figure out is how he knew my location. And how did they find us at the safe house?"

Kaleb didn't respond.

She knew he was worried she'd act rashly, so she said, "I'm not planning on taking them on alone."

He looked visibly relieved. "I'm glad to hear it. Don't get me wrong—I want this cartel taken down just as badly as you do. Easton didn't deserve to go out like he did."

Rylee settled back against the cushions on the sofa. "My gut just keeps pointing me back to Los Angeles."

"I have to ask…" Kaleb began. "Have you contacted your mother or anyone else?"

Rylee shook her head no. "Easton had me throw my cell phone away. He was going to get me another one." She paused a moment before adding, "As much as I want to talk to my mom, I haven't. The last thing I want is to put her in danger."

"That's good to hear."

"Kaleb, I don't enjoy feeling like prey or being caught off guard." She ran a finger through her hair and inhaled deeply, then released the breath slowly. Would this nightmare ever come to an end?

"Our ride is here. Wait inside," Kaleb said. He opened the door, stepped out and surveyed the area.

Rylee quickly grabbed her backpack and pulled her suitcase behind her. She waited until he signaled that it was safe for her to venture out.

She walked outside, surprised to see a taxi in the driveway.

Kaleb ushered her quickly inside the vehicle.

"I thought your brother was picking us up," she said in a low voice.

"Rylee, this is Nate."

His brother glanced over his shoulder and awarded her a friendly smile.

"You also drive a taxi?" she asked. "Kaleb said you were an architect who was a hacker and that you're also his business partner."

"This car is just a cover." Nate laughed. "My brother spoke the truth. I was in the military first. While there, I was in school studying to become an architect. I got out of the air force after I got my master's degree."

Rylee turned to Kaleb. "Your brother is an overachiever."

Laughing, Nate drove to a nearby garage and parked inside.

"We're switching cars again?" Rylee asked.

"Yeah," Kaleb responded.

They switched to another vehicle with blacked-out windows.

Glancing around, she inquired, "Where are we going?"

"To Nate's house in Whitefish Bay," Kaleb said.

"Everyone says it's beautiful there," she commented. She'd heard about it while living in Wisconsin but had never been, since she'd had to limit her movements while in WITSEC. Another reason she wanted out of the program— it wasn't like her to sit still in hiding. She needed to be out in the world again, taking down the bad guys,

"It is," Nate confirmed. "I love the area."

"Are you sure it's wise to take me to your house?" Rylee asked. "You *do* know people are looking for me." She didn't want anyone else getting hurt.

"Right now, my home is probably the safest place for you to be," Nate responded. "There's no way for anyone to connect us."

"I suppose you're right," she said.

Forty-two minutes later, they pulled into one of the garage spaces of a lakefront home on Lake View Circle in the Hoyt Park neighborhood in Whitefish Bay.

"You have a really beautiful home," Rylee stated as she looked around.

"Thanks. It was a fixer-upper that had a functional circular layout and great bones. It was perfect for the type of renovations I had in mind."

"Kaleb and I are still trying to figure out how they found you, because that place was completely off the grid. Only the three of us knew about it."

"That's what Easton told me," Rylee said.

"The only thing I can figure is that they planted a tracker on Easton somehow," Kaleb said.

She considered that. "It couldn't have been on his car. When we met up, we changed vehicles."

"Maybe they cloned his phone," Nate suggested. "Or put a GPS locator somewhere on his clothes. Either way, Easton couldn't have had any idea because he never would've knowingly led them to you."

Kaleb agreed.

"I'm grateful to you both," Rylee said. "But I think it's best to leave Wisconsin as soon as possible. They didn't find me that night, and technically I'm no longer in WITSEC, so they don't know where to look for me."

"The marshals are going to have people looking for you."

"I know but right now, we can't trust any of them. I'm safer without witness protection."

"We still have to be cautious," Kaleb said. "Calderon is not going to give up looking for you that easily."

"We can try it your way for now," Rylee stated. "But if it doesn't work—we're doing things my way."

Chapter Five

Nate gave her a tour of the formal living and dining room, the family room, and the eat-in kitchen.

"Did you decorate this place yourself or hire someone?" Rylee asked.

"I hired a friend," Nate said. "Interior design isn't a skill set I possess."

She followed him into what looked like a library. The wall was covered with shelves from ceiling to floor containing fiction and nonfiction titles. "I've always wanted a room like this," she said. "I love to read."

"It's my favorite room in the whole house," he said. "But this library is special."

"How so?" Rylee asked.

Nate walked over to one of the shelves in the middle of the wall, and suddenly a hidden door swung open to reveal a well-appointed room with twin beds, a dresser and a nightstand. It even had its own bathroom. There was a large television on the wall with views of every room in the house and another TV on top of the dresser.

"A panic room."

"We'll both be staying in here tonight," Kaleb said. "After that, we'll move you to a proper bedroom. We'll be at this house until Nate can secure new documents for you."

"Kaleb, you did a good job avoiding traffic cams," his

brother said when they returned to the family room. "I checked the route from the safe house in Milwaukee to the one in Muk-wonago. There's no reason anyone should connect the missing witness to you."

Rylee knew this was why Kaleb had had her lie down in the back seat during the drive—they didn't want her face showing up on video in case the cartel had someone monitoring traffic activity. She briefly wondered what had happened to Luis. She made a mental note to look up the accident once it was settled.

"Nate, I need you to pull the footage from that house in Milwaukee to see if we can identify the man who shot Easton."

"Will do."

She walked over to the enormous picture window in the living room and stared out. She wished the weather wasn't so cold. She yearned to enjoy the beautiful lakefront and the park they'd passed on the way to the house.

Rylee excused herself to go to the bathroom.

Glimpsing her reflection in the bright lighting, she noticed that the black tendrils surrounding her face were uneven and choppy. She hated it. She picked at the hair with her fingers, trying to even it out, but it only worsened. She let out a frustrated sigh and turned away from the mirror.

"She's not what I expected," Nate said in a low voice.

"I'm with you," Kaleb responded. "Rylee's quite a looker—beautiful enough to be a model. She's tough, though. She knows how to handle herself."

"Is she ex-military?"

Kaleb nodded. "Marines. She was working for Homeland Security before she went into WITSEC."

"Really..."

"I didn't realize what a horrible job I'd done on my hair," Rylee said when she returned, putting a pause in their discussion. "Can one of you even it up?" She had an iPad in her hand.

"Nate would do a better job than me," Kaleb responded.

She looked at his brother.

"Sure," he said.

"Let me guess…" She smiled. "You're also a part-time barber."

"Not really," he responded. "However, one of our uncles owns a chain of barbershops. He taught me how to cut hair."

He navigated to the stairs and headed up to the second level.

She looked at Kaleb and whispered, "You do know that he makes you look like a slacker?"

He laughed.

When Nate returned, Rylee pulled a chair from the dining table and sat down while he evened out her cut. She seemed focused on whatever she was doing with her tablet.

When he finished, Nate handed her a mirror.

"So much better," she murmured. "Thank you."

"You're welcome."

When Rylee went to the bathroom to shower off the excess hair, Nate said, "I like her. I can't believe she actually cut off her hair and plans to walk around in men's clothing. This is one determined woman."

"So it seems," Kaleb said.

"She's exactly your type."

Kaleb stared into eyes that were identical to his own. "Rylee is our client."

"Yes, but you can't deny you're attracted to women like her. Strong, determined and even a bit impulsive."

Rylee's sudden presence filled the room, and Kaleb couldn't

help but notice how she had changed into a comfortable ensemble of sweatpants and a long-sleeved T-shirt.

"I need a good movie," she stated, her gaze meeting his. "Something to take my mind off everything that's going on in my life right now."

Kaleb, feeling the magnetic pull between them, suggested, "How about a comedy? Laughter might be just what you need."

"That sounds perfect," she agreed, her voice holding a trace of gratitude.

As the movie played on, Kaleb couldn't help but feel a growing connection between them. With each passing moment, Rylee seemed to let her guard down, her laughter and warmth becoming more evident. It put Kaleb at ease to see her relaxing in his presence, but he cautioned himself to stay focused.

Although he was no longer with the marshals, Kaleb still worried about losing a witness. One time was more than enough for him. If only Robert Kline had listened to him. Leaving WITSEC had cost him his life.

Kaleb wasn't going to let anything happen to Rylee.

RYLEE STIFLED A YAWN. Exhaustion was quickly catching up to her. She felt a bit nervous about sleeping in the same room as Kaleb. She was struggling to keep her mind off his good looks and well-toned body.

It was a few minutes after midnight when they all decided to call it a night.

She got up and followed Kaleb to the panic room.

"I'm going to take a shower unless you need the bathroom," he announced once they were inside.

"I took mine already, so I'm fine." Rylee retrieved her iPad from her backpack, then climbed into bed to search for news of Luis's accident. It was unlikely he'd been able to drive away. She was pretty sure he'd suffered some bodily injury as well.

The Racine newspaper posted a brief mention of an accident with minor injuries, but no names were mentioned.

Rylee forced her gaze away from Kaleb and pretended to be reading when he came out of the bathroom. He wore a pair of gray sweatpants that hung low on his hips and a long-sleeved black T-shirt that was pulled tight across his chest and shoulders, showcasing toned muscles underneath. She felt the familiar pull of attraction but quickly dismissed it. No point going there.

He got into the other bed.

"Are you okay?" Kaleb asked.

After clearing her throat, Rylee answered, "Yeah. I'm fine."

"There's a heater in the corner and an electric blanket in the closet if you need them."

"Thanks."

An hour later, Rylee stole a peek at Kaleb, who appeared to be in a deep slumber.

It was obvious he took his job of protecting her very seriously. She hoped to eventually convince Kaleb to accompany her to Los Angeles. If he refused, Rylee was more than prepared to go it alone.

She needed to go back to prove that her partner hadn't been involved in trafficking drugs, and because Rylee wanted her life back. Her gut instincts told her that returning to Los Angeles was the only way to accomplish this.

She began working on a plan of action. It helped to keep her mind busy. She wasn't used to sitting and waiting on someone else to make decisions and choices for her. She hadn't had a choice with WITSEC, but now that she was on her own—she would control her narrative.

She was extremely grateful to Kaleb and Nate. She was willing to accept their help, but she *had* to return to California. Hopefully they would respect her decision.

When she could barely keep her eyes open, Rylee returned her tablet to the leather backpack then lay down, positioning her body so that her back was to Kaleb.

She didn't think she'd be able to sleep otherwise. He was so attractive in a way that she found a bit disturbing. In a good way, but the timing was bad. Her only focus right now was finding answers to two important questions: Who set up her partner, and who murdered her handler?

Chapter Six

Kaleb opened his eyes.

He'd only pretended to be asleep and was watching Rylee. A part of him worried that she might try to sneak off on her own.

She's definitely a woman on a mission.

He'd never met a woman like Rylee. She was feminine, but she wasn't the type of woman to faint or fall apart in a threatening situation. She wanted to face the danger head-on. His lips curled upward. She probably enjoyed being in control. She was agreeable thus far, but Kaleb felt this would change if she didn't get her way. Returning to Los Angeles didn't seem like a good idea to him—with new identification, Rylee could live anywhere and become invisible. But Kaleb knew she wasn't the type to run away from a fight. If he were in her shoes, he'd want to do the same thing: bring the fight to the source.

Despite his doubts, Kaleb considered Rylee's plan. She'd changed her hair and style of clothing. If she stayed away from people who knew her, she just might be able to hide in plain sight. She was no longer with Homeland Security, and he was no longer with the US Marshals Service. They were on their own. Going after the Mancuso organization... which had some of the latest technology and people in high positions loyal to it. He suspected this was how the shooters had been able to locate them, despite Rylee leaving her car behind and throwing away her cell phone before arriving at the safe house.

Rylee could probably get help from Homeland Security, but that would mean she'd have to reveal herself. The idea to tell people she'd died must've come from someone higher than her supervisor.

Kaleb's chest felt heavy with sorrow as he thought about Easton, his friend for so many years. Rage bubbled inside him like an inferno, remembering how his mentor had bravely given his life to protect Rylee. Kaleb could feel the weight of his loss pressing down on him like a boulder, and nothing could bring him relief. But as he mourned, he had to find the strength to carry on and continue the fight that had stolen Easton's life.

He was awakened by the drop in temperature a couple of hours later. He got up and grabbed two thick comforters. He tossed one on his bed and eased to where Rylee was sleeping.

She shot up, reaching for the backpack at the foot of her bed. "Has something happened?"

"No, everything's fine. I thought you might be cold." Kaleb held up the comforter. "The temperature has dropped even lower. I'm cold so I figured you might be, too."

"Oh…yes. I'll need that and the electric blanket, please."

He gave her the comforter and then went to retrieve the blanket.

"I don't know why anyone would want to live in this type of weather." She groaned. "Just doesn't seem natural."

Kaleb chuckled. "Spoken like a true West Coast native."

"See you in the morning." Rylee ducked under the covers, pulling them over her head.

KALEB WALKED INTO the kitchen the next day and found Nate cooking breakfast.

"Morning," he greeted. "I need to use one of your computers."

"You can use the one in my office. If you're looking for information on what happened to Rylee and her partner, it's already up."

He eyed Nate, then chuckled as he accepted the cup of coffee his brother offered. "I don't know how you do that, but it's kinda scary."

"C'mon, I've been doing this all our lives," Nate responded. "You should be used to it now. By the way, I couldn't see anything on the video from the house in Milwaukee. There were three men, but their faces were covered up. No way to identify the third guy."

"Great."

Kaleb strode out the kitchen and walked down the hall to his brother's office to read what had happened when Rylee and her partner were shot. He was shocked to find that the man who'd died that night was found with millions of dollars in his account and drugs in the house. The investigation looked to be an open case still.

"HSI isn't completely convinced that Stuart Houston is guilty of anything," he said to himself.

He heard Rylee in the kitchen talking to Nate. When he'd gotten up earlier, she was still buried under the mountain of bed coverings. She must have woken shortly after he left the room.

Kaleb closed the page and left to join them for breakfast.

Rylee pointed to the omelet and sliced potatoes covered in onions and green and red peppers. "Nate, you're a man of *many* talents, I see. This looks very delicious."

"Thanks." His brother shrugged. "I enjoy cooking."

"Why haven't you been snatched up already?" Rylee asked.

Nate offered a smile. "I suppose it's because I haven't met Mrs. Right yet."

Her gaze briefly scanned Kaleb, who'd been silently observing their exchange.

His face must've shown concern, because she asked, "What is it?"

"I'm sure you know that there's some pretty strong evidence linking your partner to the Mancuso organization…"

"It's not true." She shook her head. "Stuart is an innocent victim." Her tone brooked no argument.

Kaleb understood her loyalty to her partner, but Rylee had to consider the possibility that Stuart Houston wasn't the man she thought him to be.

"I know what you're thinking," she stated, sending him a sharp glare. "Stuart wasn't dirty. He was set up."

"Why *him*?" Kaleb asked.

"I don't have an answer for you," she responded. "There are missing pieces to this puzzle for sure. It's why I want to get back out there."

"But the evidence against him—"

"You don't know Stuart," she cut him off. "He didn't live beyond his means. At best, he was frugal. But more than that—my partner wouldn't be involved in drug trafficking. His mother died of a heroin overdose when he was fifteen. It's why he joined the agency. I joined for a similar reason— my younger brother had a cocaine addiction." She paused momentarily, then added, "Now that we're here, I think we need to discuss a plan of action."

"The first thing is to get you some new identification," Kaleb responded. "We'll stay here until the documents are ready."

"That's fine," she murmured. "But what are we doing after that?"

"Let's just take it one day at a time."

"I haven't changed my mind about Los Angeles," Rylee said. "I hope you'll come with me, but I understand if you decide not to."

Kaleb sighed. "Have you considered reaching out to Homeland Security?"

"Yes. I need them. I also think we need the help of some of the other agencies as well. Like DEA and ATF…even the FBI. Especially if we want to start tearing down the Mancuso organization. It needs to be a joint task force operation."

Nate didn't bother to hide his grin.

Kaleb picked up his glass of juice and took a long sip. "I see you've been giving this a lot of thought." He wasn't surprised by this. Rylee wasn't one to just sit on the sidelines.

"I have," she said. "I need answers. I don't understand why Stuart decided to chase down a lead that had nothing to do with any of our investigations. We were working a money laundering investigation at the time. I have to find out why he didn't just hand it off to the agent looking into the Mancuso cartel."

Kaleb nodded in agreement.

"If I may jump in here," Nate said. "It sounds like there was possibly an informant—someone within the cartel. Calderon might have suspected a trap, so he fed that person the wrong information. I would bet that person is dead. We should check to see if any other bodies showed up near that area in the days following the shooting."

She'd replayed that night over and over in her mind. When she and her partner fell victim to an ambush and gunfire, the memories etched themselves deeply, creating a haunting recollection of tragedy. The chaos, the relentless sound of bullets and the agonizing sight of her wounded partner by her side were imprinted vividly on her brain. That fateful night had left an indelible mark on her soul. The weight of guilt and grief bore down on her as she'd entered the witness protection program. She had to bid farewell to her former life, her name and her past. Since that night, she kept trying to peel back the layers, but there was nothing that stood out.

"I want to get to the bottom of this just as much as you do," Kaleb said. "Nobody has been able to really infiltrate that organization. DEA's gotten a couple of their members on some of the smaller charges, but those guys aren't talking. They're willing to do the time."

Rylee nodded in agreement. "They were more afraid of Raul's wrath than prison. Now that he's dead, they don't want to anger Calderon. We need some solid intel and major arrests to put a hole in that organization's armor. It's going to take a joint task force operation dedicated to taking down this cartel."

"If the cartel was able to place a mole in the marshals' office, whoever's running this task force will need to personally vet each team member," Nate said.

"Exactly," Rylee responded.

Kaleb gave a slight nod. "I agree."

The more he got to know Rylee, the more he wanted to help her. Still, Kaleb had to convince her to be patient. He had a feeling the cartel wouldn't just give up. They'd made the first move, and they would make another.

There were several people in the marshals' service who knew of his close relationship with Easton. He expected that someone would reach out to him about Rylee. Kaleb had already determined that the best way to keep her safe was to deny knowing of her existence. Allow everyone to believe she'd taken off on her own. It wasn't that far from the truth.

RYLEE WASN'T SURE whether Kaleb and Nate believed her where Stuart was concerned, which made her that much more determined to prove his innocence.

She sat there watching the two brothers interacting and felt a twinge of sadness. Rylee's heart ached as the memories of her brother overwhelmed her with grief and longing. The war on drugs seemed like an unwinnable battle, with no end in sight. But she refused to give up; her determination to fight for justice was unshakable, a promise that would remain until her final breath.

She knew that same drive to do right existed in Kaleb. His loyalty to Easton in keeping his word to his friend was a quality she admired. Her gaze slid over his athletic frame before she forced her eyes elsewhere. She released a soft sigh, determined to keep her emotions under control. Her primary focus had to be on staying alive. She could tell that Kaleb and Nate were extremely close from their interactions with one another. Both men possessed a protective nature—which was probably why they'd decided to open a private security firm.

A smile formed on her lips as she listened to the light bantering between them.

Nate glanced over at her. "Are you a sports fan?"

"I am," she responded. "Basketball. I'm a die-hard Lakers fan."

"What did I tell you?" Kaleb said with a chuckle.

"How did you know?" Rylee asked.

"The purple-and-gold socks you're wearing and the key chain on your backpack," he responded. "Also, the gold basketball jersey with *Lakers* emblazoned on it."

"That was a lucky guess," she responded. "I also have a vintage Seattle Supersonics—my dad was a huge fan—and a Milwaukee Bucks jersey."

"Yeah, but now you feel safe enough to wear your Lakers gear," Kaleb stated. "You have the others just as part of your cover."

"I almost forgot that you were a marshal."

Nate chuckled. "I keep telling my brother that he should consider going back into law enforcement. He's got good instincts, and besides…he loved it."

"It's time to change the subject," Kaleb said.

Rylee glimpsed the emotion in his eyes. "Do you miss being a marshal?"

"There are times," he answered. "But Nate and I have our own company now."

"Which I can run," his brother interjected. "I've even offered to buy him out whenever he's ready to go back to law enforcement."

"Speaking of which…did Easton promise to pay you for helping me?" Rylee asked. "I have some money in my savings, but it probably doesn't come close to what you usually charge."

"No," Kaleb responded. "This is a friend doing another friend a favor."

"Are you sure?"

He looked at her. "Positive."

"I was just beginning to believe that Racine was far enough to escape Calderon's grasp. I won't make that mistake again." Rylee got up, walked to a nearby window and stared outside. After a few minutes, she closed the blinds, moved to the door and ensured it was locked.

Although she wasn't technically in danger at this moment, she'd never truly feel safe.

Not until Calderon was in custody.

KALEB SHIFTED HIS gaze to Rylee. Being in such close quarters for an unspecified amount of time amplified the attraction, and Kaleb's heart raced. He forced his eyes back to his plate, but all he could think of was her almond-shaped eyes and full lips. He wanted nothing more than to lean in and kiss her, but there was no way they could explore their chemistry—not while someone out there wanted her dead.

Nate got up, offering to clear their plates, and left the room with the dishes shortly after. Kaleb needed to tell her about the call he'd received earlier that day. "Easton's funeral is on Friday. I'm going to pay my respects… I was asked to speak about him."

Rylee shifted her position on the sofa. "I wish I could go with you. I feel like I owe him that much."

He nodded. "He tried hard to convince me to stay with the marshals, but I didn't have the heart for it. He wasn't only my mentor and friend. He was also a surrogate father to me."

"I'm so sorry for your loss, Kaleb… If you can, please tell Easton farewell for me." She released a soft sigh. "I hate that he died keeping me safe. If only he'd let me back him up…"

"You might have been killed along with him. He didn't want that."

She gave a slight nod. "Be careful at the funeral."

"I will."

She put down her mug. "Be honest with me. Can some-one find me here? Is there something you're not telling me?"

"No," Kaleb responded. "We took every precaution to ensure we weren't followed."

"Are the marshals looking for me?"

"They are most likely trying to find you. They will want to assign you a new handler."

"I don't trust that. Not with a leak in the agency."

"Neither do I," he responded. "I think you should let Easton's superior know that you're alive, but you've left WITSEC."

Rylee nodded in agreement. "I think you're right. It's

enough to keep out of sight from the cartel. I need to stay invisible."

"That's why we need to get you some new identification. I know you want to go back to Los Angeles, but I think we should wait until after Easton's funeral."

"I know you want to pay your respects and say goodbye," Rylee responded, "but I hope you'll also be paying close attention to the other guests in attendance."

Kaleb nodded. "That's the plan."

Maybe it was all the drama of the past few days and the amount of sleep she was currently running on, but Rylee lost some of her patience. "As far as getting a new ID… I'm not changing my name again. I don't care what it says on paper—I'm staying Rylee Greenwood."

"We should change your last name," he responded.

"I hope I don't sound ungrateful, Kaleb. I appreciate all you and Nate are doing for me, but if the cartel can track me so easily, it won't matter what I call myself. You know this as well as I do."

"The ID will help while we're traveling. They will be looking for Rylee Greenwood or Rolanda Green."

She considered his words, then said, "I see your point. I'm willing to do whatever to stay above ground. I can't take down the Mancuso cartel if I'm dead."

Chapter Seven

Kaleb drove into the parking lot of the Holy Name of Jesus Church in Racine and parked in a space a few yards from the entrance.

Inside, he approached a slender woman with skin the color of warm chocolate. He embraced Easton's wife. "Sylvia, my condolences…"

"Thank you so much for coming," she said. "It's good to see you, Kaleb."

"I hate that it's under these circumstances. I'm sorry for your loss."

"My father died doing what he loved," a young woman said, joining them. "Hello, Kaleb." Deputy Marshal Nova Bennett swiped her curly hair away from her face.

He hugged her. "Good to see you."

"Good to see you, too."

"I hope you know Easton was very proud of you."

"Thank you for saying that." He made small talk with the two women until Sylvia excused herself to speak to one of the funeral directors.

"Word on the street is the Mancuso cartel is behind my father's murder. They aren't making this public, but they found a GPS tracker in his shoe," Nova stated in a low voice. "That's how they were able to locate him."

Kaleb glanced around to make sure they weren't overheard.

"Easton believed there was a mole inside the agency. That's why he reached out to me for help."

Nova's eyes widened in surprise. "He could've come to me."

"Your father wouldn't have done that—he would never put your life at risk. Nova, I don't have to tell you how important it is for you to say nothing where your father is concerned."

"I understand. Just let me know what I can do to help."

He knew she wanted to inquire about the witness but did not. Nova was aware that there were too many people around to discuss Rylee, although Kaleb wasn't sure how much she knew about her father's witness or how much he should tell her.

"All is well," he said in a voice low enough for her ears alone.

Nova gave him a tiny smile. "Be careful."

"I will," he promised.

"Thank you for coming," she said, loud enough for those around them to hear.

Kaleb gave a slight nod. "I wouldn't be anywhere else." He gestured toward the doors leading to the sanctuary. "I guess I'd better get inside."

She pasted on a smile. "I'll see you later at the repast, right?"

"Yes, I'll be there."

As he turned away, he felt the hair at the back of his neck stand up.

Kaleb's gaze scanned the room. His eyes landed on a young woman standing a few feet away from him. She stood there boldly watching him.

When the woman realized she'd captured his attention, she smiled.

He offered her a polite smile in return before a few of his former coworkers came over to talk to him.

But Kaleb could still feel the woman's eyes on him. He was used to receiving such attentiveness from women over the years, but he had yet to find the one woman to share his life with. Few women could tolerate what he did for a living.

He thought of Rylee. Now, she was something else. She wasn't the type of woman who would get weak at the knees or faint away under the threat of danger. He liked that about her.

With a quickened pace, Kaleb made his way to his seat, knowing that the service was about to commence. The hairs on the nape of his neck prickled with an unsettling alertness, and he couldn't dispel the sensation that someone had their eyes on him.

Turning his head to the left, he locked eyes with John Martin, a figure from his past, once his partner at the US marshals' agency. If John had any involvement in Easton's demise or posed a threat to Rylee's safety...

Kaleb pushed that worrisome thought aside as the music signaled the beginning of the service.

AFTER THE FUNERAL, Kaleb hung back, observing the agency staff in attendance. He noticed that John Martin was wearing an expensive watch and clothing. He also noted the costly designer purse his wife carried.

Amidst the somber atmosphere, Kaleb stood with a heavy heart. Memories of his and Easton's shared experiences at the agency flooded Kaleb's mind, and a deep sense of loss settled in his chest. He felt a profound gratitude for his friendship with Easton and made a solemn vow to honor the memory of his departed comrade.

The young woman who'd been watching him earlier sashayed up to him. "What you said up there was just beautiful. It was a moving tribute..."

She had spent much of the service trying to catch Kaleb's

eye rather than listening respectfully to the words spoken about his friend. It had irritated him.

"Yes, it was," another woman in a formfitting green dress said when she joined them. She put on a bright smile for Kaleb. "Hello, I don't think we've ever met. I'm Brenda Perez. I work with the US Marshals Service as an administrative assistant. I overheard a couple of people saying that you used to work for the agency, so it's really nice to meet you."

Visibly irritated, the younger woman stalked away.

"You looked like you needed rescuing," she said in a loud whisper.

"No, I'm good," he responded casually. "I'm Kaleb, by the way."

Brenda shook his hand. "From what you said during your speech, you and Easton must have a long history."

"We do."

"It's so terrible what happened. When I first heard the news, I cried like nobody's business."

"I think we're all still in shock."

"I know I am," Brenda replied. "I heard one person say they thought it might have been his witness who did it. No one knows where she is or what happened to her. Other people say that she was also killed, but they just haven't found her body. I also heard that the footage from the safe house showed the shooter leaving alone that night. This is just so tragic."

Kaleb eyed her. "What do you know about this witness?"

"Only what I've heard."

"How long have you been with the marshals' service?"

"About three years now. I think you must have just left when I got the job."

"Then you've been there long enough to know that you shouldn't go around talking about anything you've heard at work. Especially to people you don't know."

Her smile disappeared. "You're right. I hope you won't say anything. I really need to keep my job. I never would've said anything if you hadn't worked there."

"I'm not a marshal anymore. I own a private security firm."

"Oh wow… I'm impressed."

Kaleb caught sight of John Martin and his wife. They looked like they were about to leave for the repast. His former partner was always a frugal man. He wondered where the influx of wealth had come from.

Brenda pulled him out of his observing by asking, "Do you happen to have a business card on you?"

Kaleb reached into his jacket pocket and handed her one. "It was nice meeting you, Brenda. I'm afraid I need to leave."

"Are you going to the repast? If so, I'll see you there."

He smiled. "I'll be there."

Kaleb walked away without looking back. He knew she was watching him—he could feel the weight of her gaze. But he needed to get to the repast—maybe he'd learn something about the leak. He needed to focus his attention on John.

Chapter Eight

Nate was in his office working, so Rylee sat in the family room with her iPad. She reviewed the notes she'd written to remember everything that happened the night she and Stuart were ambushed.

Rylee recalled asking Stuart how he'd obtained the tip, and he'd responded that he preferred to keep his contact's name a secret. Maybe Nate was right. Maybe it was someone with a grudge against Calderon.

It suddenly came back to her that she'd had a bad feeling that day, but she'd trusted her partner, so she'd dismissed it. Stuart had a reputation for being very thorough when it came to investigating leads.

"Why didn't you tell me everything?" Rylee whispered. "I'm pulling at straws here…trying to clear your name for your family. I know you weren't dirty and I intend to prove it."

She spent the next couple of hours reading articles surrounding the cartel.

Rylee glanced at the clock, rose to her feet and walked over to the fireplace. She felt a wave of sadness flow through her at the thought of the Bennett family having to deal with Easton's death because of her. If she'd known that he would be killed, Rylee would've attempted to handle Luis alone.

Her eyes strayed back to the clock. The service was probably almost over by now. Kaleb had mentioned that he'd planned to stop by his house afterward before heading back.

She didn't want to admit to herself that she missed him. Nor did she want to acknowledge just how much she was looking forward to his return.

It was snowing outside.

Rylee walked over to the window for a closer look. Snow made everything look beautiful and magical, especially during the holidays, but she'd had enough of it to last a lifetime.

"Feel free to go out there and make a snowman."

She glanced over her shoulder at Nate. "No, thank you. That thought never once occurred to me. I was thinking how much I want sunshine and hot weather."

"I can understand that. There are times when I want those things, too. But then on days like this, I enjoy watching the falling snow. I was just about to make some hot chocolate. You want some?"

"Yes, thank you," Rylee responded. "I'm enjoying the heat from this fireplace. I've been in Wisconsin for fifteen months, but my body still hasn't adjusted to the weather."

"It takes some getting used to," Nate said. "Especially if you didn't grow up in a cold climate." He handed her a cup of the warm liquid a few moments later along with a sandwich.

"Thank you," Rylee said. "I know some people complain about the heat in California and Nevada, but it's never bothered me."

Her eyes strayed to the clock again.

"Kaleb shouldn't be gone too much longer."

She gave a stiff nod, embarrassed over being caught. Rylee wondered if he could discern that she was experiencing some unsettled emotions where his brother was concerned.

Rylee sighed, her fingers trembling as she picked up a pickle. Her heart ached as she thought about the funerals she had missed—first Stuart's and now Easton's. She wished more than anything that she had been able to say goodbye to them, to let them know how much they meant to her. But now it was too late.

"I can imagine how frustrating this has been for you," Nate stated. "To have your life turned upside down."

"It's been challenging at times. I loved my job with HSI. Mostly, I hate not being able to talk to my mother. I miss her so much. She was not just Mom…she was also my best friend." Her heart sank a little, and she felt her eyes fill with tears. She blinked rapidly.

Nate eyed her. "I know that's hard on you both."

Rylee said, "The other thing is that Stuart's wife and children need to know that he wasn't working for the cartel— that's just not true."

"Have you considered the possibility that maybe your partner was forced to participate?"

"He wouldn't have done it," Rylee stated.

"Not even to save his family?" Nate asked.

"If he were in trouble, I think Stuart would've told me."

"Raul Mancuso had been known to kidnap family members to force someone's hand. Word on the streets is that Calderon uses the exact same method to get what he wants."

"Stuart and I had a code word if something like that ever happened. As far as I know, Elena and the children were never threatened or kidnapped," Rylee responded. "I know that Stuart's innocent, Nate. I have always trusted my gut. I know someone framed him."

He smiled. "I have no doubt you'll get to the bottom of this."

She wiped her mouth on the edge of her napkin. "I'm going to give it my best."

THE REPAST WAS held at the home Easton and Sylvia had shared for over thirty years. Kaleb remembered vividly the last time he'd visited the couple six months ago—they had surprised him with a birthday dinner in his honor.

Kaleb walked into the house, feeling the weight of his grief pressing down on him. A heavy silence hung in the air, only the sound of his footsteps breaking it.

Sylvia sat in the armchair by the fireplace, her eyes fixed on the dancing flames. She looked so small, so vulnerable, and Kaleb's heart ached to see her like this. From the heart-broken expression on her face, the reality of Easton's death had finally sunk in.

"Do you need anything?" he asked softly, approaching her.

"I can't believe he's gone," she replied, her voice barely above a whisper. "Life will never be the same for me."

Kaleb took a seat across from her.

They sat in silence for a few moments, lost in their own thoughts. The room was filled with memories of Easton; photographs of their life together hung on the walls, and favorite pieces of furniture they had collected over the years were scattered throughout the house.

"I miss him so much," Sylvia said, breaking the silence.

"I know," Kaleb said, reaching for her hand. "I miss him, too. He was a good man."

She nodded, tears streaming down her face.

Her daughter joined them.

"Mama, you should try to eat," Nova said. "I can have a plate fixed for you."

Sylvia shook her head. "I don't have an appetite. I'll try to eat something later."

Kaleb saw the sadness in Nova's eyes as they lingered on the photos of her father that had been carefully placed along the mantel. He knew how much she had loved her dad, and losing him so suddenly must have been unbearable for her. Kaleb was desperate to find some words that could bring her solace, but he knew nothing he said would make it better.

He rose to his feet. He wanted to give Sylvia and Nova some time alone, so he joined the guests gathered in the dining room.

"Would you like me to make a plate for you?" Brenda asked. "I don't mind doing it."

"I'm fine," he responded.

Kaleb continued on toward the family room and spotted John, one of his least favorite people.

John met Kaleb's gaze head-on and with what felt like a sly grin said, "It's been a while."

Kaleb responded with a curt nod and a quiet acknowledgment that it had.

"I heard you started your own business."

"I did."

"A security firm, I think," John stated.

He nodded.

"Easton mentioned it a while back. How's it going?"

Kaleb offered a slight smile. "I can't complain. Business is good."

"Glad to hear it," John responded.

"I didn't think you cared."

John's brow lifted. "I thought we cleared the air before you left the agency." Their varied approaches to handling cases, enforcing the law and managing workloads had created a lot of tension between the two men.

"We did," Kaleb said. "But I still don't like you."

John chuckled. "The feeling is mutual."

Kaleb's eyes traveled the length of the room and landed on Brenda. She stood across the room watching him, her expression unreadable.

Turning back to John, he said, "I see you've acquired a sense of fashion. That suit looks like classic Dior."

"It is," John responded with a grin. "My wife gave it to me during our anniversary trip to Morocco."

"Sounds extravagant," Kaleb stated.

"We stayed at this magnificent five-star resort in Marrakech…"

John bragged about toasting his wedding anniversary with a $900 bottle of champagne.

"Did you win the lottery or something?"

John eyed him, then gestured to his left. "I'd better go see what the wife wants." When the Martins picked up their coats and made the rounds saying goodbye, Kaleb hastily said goodbye to Sylvia, then rushed out to his car.

He didn't want to lose sight of the Martins—he wanted to find out more. He followed them to a prestigious gated neighborhood on Milwaukee's east side. The original English Tudor style of the house with its red ashlar sandstone brick could be seen, and it sat on a corner lot facing Lake Park.

How can John afford this place? The houses in this neighborhood started at around $2.5 million. He knew this because he had a client who lived in the area. This was clearly outside of a marshal's salary.

Kaleb felt a bitter taste as he thought about Easton and how he'd died. John had always been the type to blur the lines of the law, and with his sudden wealth…

He sat there a minute before driving away.

After ensuring he didn't have a tail, Kaleb returned to Whitefish Bay.

During the drive, he thought about what Nova had told him—someone had planted a device in her father's shoe. Easton kept an extra pair of shoes at the agency, and he often went to the gym after his shift. From the clothes he'd been wearing when Kaleb last saw him, it looked like he'd either been heading to or leaving the gym when Rylee reached out to him.

Raul was rumored to have been a very paranoid man. It was said that he had his place swept for bugs daily and didn't like to talk business over the phone. It was also rumored that he'd gone as far as to hire someone to be his double.

Yet he was dead, too.

Officially, his death was caused by an unknown assailant, but rumors were rampant that he'd been murdered by the one person he trusted most in his life—Calderon.

Kaleb wanted to dismantle the Mancuso organization as much as Rylee did. He knew Nova wanted to see those responsible for her father's death punished as well. Easton's daughter would be patient for now, but Rylee...

She wanted to rush back to Los Angeles to try and take down the man she held responsible for killing her partner and shooting her. She was reluctant to accept the possibility that Stuart could have been involved with the cartel—he could've gotten in over his head. Unfortunately, it happened sometimes.

As he neared his brother's house, Kaleb was excited about occupying the same space with Rylee. He had noticed the spark between them, but his duty as a protector weighed heavily on him. Any thought of pursuing anything more than friendship with her seemed foolish and irresponsible.

Robert Kline was the last person Kaleb was assigned to in WITSEC—and he'd decided to leave the program when his wife announced she wanted a divorce. He was dead within a week of blowing his own cover.

Kaleb had tried to convince him to stay, but the man was determined to abandon WITSEC. After Kline's death, Kaleb was haunted by the question of whether he'd done all he could.

Rylee was as stubborn as Kline, but this time Kaleb vowed to keep the person in his custody safe by any means necessary.

KALEB'S BEING AWAY fed the edginess that had been with Rylee for the past couple of days.

She decided to get some exercise, so she ventured to the workout room. Exercising had a way of helping to clear her mind.

Rylee stretched before getting on the treadmill.

Next, she decided to work on her core with light weights.

Every now and then, Rylee would glance at the clock.

After her workout, she took a shower.

Ten minutes later, Rylee walked into the family room dressed in jeans and a sweatshirt.

She went back to the living room, sat down on the sofa and turned the television to a music channel.

Minutes later, Rylee rose to her feet expectantly when Kaleb entered the house, saying, "I hadn't planned to be gone so long, but there was something I needed to check out. I also wanted to make sure I wasn't followed back here."

"How was the service?" she asked.

"It was nice," he responded. "Easton was well-liked and respected by everyone. The people that spoke shared things about him I never knew."

"Did anything or anyone stand out?"

Kaleb removed his blazer before taking a seat. "One of the marshals, John Martin, had on a suit that I know had to cost his entire monthly salary. The Vacheron Constantin watch he was wearing had to set him back about forty grand."

Settling down on the sofa, Rylee eyed him. "You certainly seem to know your brands. The only watches I've ever owned were all Timex."

"I love watches," he explained. "I have a collection…some antiques, but nothing that costs a tenth of that."

"That's very interesting," she murmured.

"You should've seen the car he was driving. A Maserati Levante. When I worked with John, he drove an old Audi 6 and his wife drove a van. They lived in a small but nice house ten miles from the job." Removing his tie, Kaleb added, "His wife was also draped in designer clothing from head to toe. I noticed that he upgraded her simple gold band to a wedding set with a huge rock in the middle. I'd say it had to be a good four carats. He was always on the shady side, so I wouldn't be surprised if it turned out that he was the leak."

Frowning, Rylee questioned, "Did Easton ever mention anything to you about him? I'm sure he noticed his co-worker's sudden wealth."

"Not really," Kaleb responded. "He couldn't stand John, so he rarely came up in our conversations."

"So, what is his story?" she asked.

"I asked if he'd won the lottery but didn't get a response. It's pretty easy to check out."

If John was the mole, he was a detriment to the marshals' service. No witness would be safe.

"There's been gossip for years about John being shady, so I'm sure someone has looked into his finances," Kaleb said. "Apparently, there weren't any red flags."

"Maybe they didn't go deep enough," Rylee suggested.

Kaleb agreed. "John's a jerk and he's no stranger to crossing lines."

Rylee nodded. "Easton mentioned there was one person in the agency he thought might be the leak, but he didn't mention a name. From what you've said about this John Martin, he was probably talking about him."

"Maybe he couldn't resist the money," Nate stated. "It

sounds like he's financially stable now, so losing his job wouldn't be a big deal."

"If John has gone this far…I'm sure he already has an escape plan," Rylee said. "He could already be under investigation."

"True," Kaleb responded. "But I don't get the sense that he is. I didn't get that vibe from anyone earlier at the funeral. He and his coworkers were talking and laughing like old friends."

Rylee met his gaze. "Maybe this goes higher than John."

"Let's just start with him and see where it takes us."

"Agreed," she murmured.

When Kaleb's eyes met hers, Rylee's heart turned over in response. She was flattered by his interest. She was keenly aware that he ignited a gently growing fire within.

Once again, Rylee reminded herself to stay focused. She couldn't allow her emotions to get carried away.

Chapter Nine

Rylee and Kaleb watched hours of footage, but none of the Martins' visitors were linked to the Mancuso cartel.

"John's phone records also don't connect him in any way," he said.

"He could have a burner phone," Rylee suggested. She wasn't ready to admit that they might be wrong about John.

"He has several conversations with his stockbroker, but I'm sure he didn't make all that money through investments," Kaleb stated.

"We did find out that John has an account in the Cayman Islands," Nate interjected.

"He's hiding money," she murmured, her head bent as she studied her hands.

Nate nodded in agreement. "Most likely from the IRS. He might also want financial privacy. It's not a crime to deposit money in international banks as long as the person is in compliance with US tax laws."

"I'm more interested in the source of his wealth," Kaleb said.

"Sounds like he's pretty flashy with it—that's for sure," Rylee interjected. "But I have to wonder why he'd be so bold if the money was illegal? As much as I'd like to connect this man to the cartel...that part just doesn't make sense to me.

I'm beginning to think that we're grasping at straws. I'm not sure we'll find any answers."

"What are you saying?" Kaleb asked. He watched Rylee's face as emotions raced across it.

"I can't stand sitting here feeling so helpless. I have to consider that as much as I want to win, we may not catch a break." Rylee shook her head in dismay.

He eyed her. "You like being in control."

Rylee felt a tad bit offended by his comment. "I'm not sure I'd say that," she responded tersely.

Kaleb cocked his head to one side. "Nothing wrong with it—as long as you recognize there are just some things that will be completely out of your control."

"I know that…" Rylee looked at him. "Do you really think I'm a control addict?"

"Just a little," he answered.

She swallowed hard but offered Kaleb a tiny smile. "Maybe I am…*a little*."

His gaze was as soft as a caress. "Like I said, it's not a bad thing."

Rylee flattened her palms on her denim-clad lap. "I never thought it was—I considered it a necessity."

Kaleb chuckled.

"I need a mental break," Rylee announced, getting up to stretch. "I just want to enjoy the rest of the day without focusing on anything else."

"I think that's a good idea. You're stressing yourself out trying to figure out everything."

"So, can we go out to eat?" she asked.

"No," Kaleb responded. "But we can have a delicious meal from a nice restaurant delivered to the house."

Rylee sighed. "I guess that will have to do."

"I've ordered dinner for the three of us," Kaleb told Nate a few minutes later when he joined them.

"I have some work to do," Nate said. "You two enjoy without me."

Kaleb eyed him. "It won't hurt you to eat with us."

"Fine, I'll join you, but you're not going to be able to hide behind me all the time, little brother."

"I don't know what you're talking about, Nate."

Heading to the door, Nate said, "I'm going upstairs to shower."

Kaleb wondered if Rylee could sense his growing attraction to her. He hoped not. Neither of them could afford to be distracted while trying to prevent another tragedy. He regretted telling Easton that he was in the middle of something—he should've postponed his dinner meeting and left to meet his friend at the safe house. Maybe Easton would still be alive.

He'd assumed they would be safe until he could get to them.

He was wrong.

Rylee was tired of being inside the house, but Kaleb wasn't going to become complacent.

Going forward, they all had to use extreme caution.

SHE CHECKED OUT her reflection in the full-length mirror. Rylee fluffed her curly tendrils with her fingers.

Why do I care about the way I look? Am I doing this for Kaleb?

Rylee dared not answer. Her life was in danger. She had lost everything that mattered to her before and now, she was close to losing it again. The truth was she had nothing to offer him.

Kaleb and his brother had compromised their own safety to protect her. She was nothing more than a client—there wasn't any point in looking for something more from him.

She drew in a deep breath and exhaled before exiting the bedroom.

Rylee pasted on a smile when she strolled downstairs and into the living room. "Has the food arrived?"

"Yeah, and I'm hungry," Kaleb said, leading the way to the dining room.

She found that Kaleb had ordered food and Nate had set the table.

Rylee glanced around, checking out her surroundings. "Oh wow...this is beautiful."

Nate arranged the containers of food in the center of the table. "Wait until you taste the food."

"It smells delicious," she responded. "I can't wait to try the shrimp po'boy. And the buffalo cauliflower bites appetizer."

Nate blessed the food.

Rylee sampled her sandwich. "This is so good."

Kaleb, Rylee and Nate sat around the table, their faces reflecting a mixture of exhaustion and determination. As they shared a meal, the conversation was laced with an unspoken camaraderie that had grown stronger through adversity. The clinking of utensils and hushed exchanges provided a temporary respite from the constant threat looming outside, reminding them of the bonds forged in the crucible of their existence. The walls held secrets, but they had each other's trust, and in that fragile moment, it was enough for Rylee to temporarily forget that someone was out to kill her.

After dinner, Kaleb said, "Nate checked the video from the night of Easton's murder and came up with nothing. They had their faces covered. However, one of them appeared to be limping. He also had a sling on. Something was wrong with his arm."

"That has to be Luis," Rylee murmured. "He's the one who showed up at my job. The way he looked at me when standing at the bar—I got a real bad feeling. I thought I might be overreacting but couldn't wait to leave. I was glad when he was seated in the restaurant. I'd planned to be gone before the server took his order. But when I left work, he followed me. I was able to get away from him by running a red light. He was hit by another car trying to come after me."

"It's good you were able to get away," Nate said.

Rylee nodded in agreement.

KALEB REALLY LIKED RYLEE. She radiated a vitality that drew him like a magnet. He had to remind himself that she was a client, but his feelings for her had nothing to do with reason.

He could feel his brother's eyes on him. Kaleb looked at Nate and offered a tiny smile.

"Just another day or so before the new ID comes in," he said. "I still don't think you should return to LA, though."

"I know you don't, but you'll have to trust me. While they are looking for me in Wisconsin, I'll be halfway to California."

When they finished eating, they kept talking over their drinks.

"You're probably going to laugh at me when I tell you that I had a great time tonight," Rylee stated. "I know I sound like I've never been anywhere."

"We get it," Nate responded.

Kaleb's phone rang, but he didn't recognize the number. "Hello…"

"This is Brenda Perez. Um…we met at Easton's funeral."

"I didn't really think I'd hear from you this soon," Kaleb said. "I honestly thought you were just being polite."

"I felt that we sort of hit it off, so I called to see if you'd be available for drinks tomorrow."

Kaleb held back his thoughts and tilted his head to catch a

glimpse of Rylee. He shifted his feet and said quietly, "Sure. What time?" Maybe getting to know Brenda would lead to identifying the source of the leak in the agency.

"After work. There's a nice little bar near my home. I'll text you the exact time and address."

"Great."

"I'm looking forward to seeing you again."

"Same," Kaleb replied.

"Who was that?" Nate asked when his brother ended the call.

"That was Brenda…the woman I met at Easton's funeral. She's an administrative assistant with the agency. She just invited me to have drinks."

"Sounds like you've got yourself a date," Rylee said.

"It's nothing like that," he stated. "The only reason I agreed to meet with her is to learn more about John."

"You think you can get information from this lady?" Nate asked.

"She's talkative."

"She sounds pretty thirsty to me," Rylee muttered.

Nate chuckled.

She leaned back in her chair. "Make sure you pay. If she pays, she'll be expecting more from you."

Kaleb clenched his jaw. "That's not gonna happen. I'm on a fact-finding mission."

Rylee laughed. "Is she pretty?"

Studying her expression, Kaleb thought he detected a hint of something but couldn't be sure. "She's nice-looking."

"Well, enjoy your evening." Rylee slipped out of her chair and walked away.

"If I didn't know better, I'd say she was jealous," Nate whispered when she was out of hearing range.

"Naw…" Kaleb responded. "She's not interested in me like

that. The moment she has an opportunity, Rylee will head to Los Angeles without so much as a goodbye." He'd made a vow to protect Rylee, but as time passed, it became more and more difficult for him to keep. His attraction intensified every day, and he wasn't sure which way to turn.

"I disagree," Nate said. "She's focused and smart. Rylee knows that she needs our help."

"You think we should?"

"Yeah. She can't get to Los Angeles without us covering her back. From everything we've learned, the answers are back there."

Kaleb responded, "I can get her there safely, but what's next?"

"She's going to have to talk to Homeland Security," Nate responded. "She'll need their help as well."

"I thought so, too," Kaleb said. "But even with a special task force, it's not going to be easy to take down the Mancuso cartel."

"Not necessarily…" Nate responded. "You just need the right information to lead to a major bust."

He considered his brother's words.

"You'd rather Rylee stay here in Wisconsin?" Nate asked.

"I think she's safer here than back in LA," Kaleb said. "I'm surprised you don't agree with me."

"I do, but it's Rylee's decision," Nate responded. "People like her, you can't tell them anything. They're determined to get their own way. At least she knows how to take care of herself."

"Yeah."

"I need to run background checks on some potential new hires," Nate said. "I'll be in my office."

"I should be helping you."

"You've got your hands full. I'll let you know if I need help."

Kaleb went to join Rylee in the family room. Falling for her would make Kaleb overly protective—something Rylee probably wouldn't appreciate, but if he kept his emotions in check, he might come across as cold and push her away.

She was special; she had the power to make Kaleb forget everything else around him. "You look tense," he said. "If you want, I can give you a neck and shoulder massage."

"Sure," she responded. "I'd like that."

He pulled out a chair. "Sit here."

She did as he requested.

Kaleb placed both hands on her shoulders and gently began massaging by pressing both thumbs down.

"That feels nice," Rylee murmured. "I can feel the stress leaving my body."

The feel of her skin sent warm tremors through Kaleb's body. He couldn't ignore the intense physical awareness between them. He struggled to resist the temptation to plant a kiss on her neck. No matter what happened, keeping her safe was paramount.

Kaleb had to force himself to stop. His desire to touch her overrode everything else.

She turned to face him. "Thank you. I feel so much better now."

"That's what I enjoy hearing."

"I'm going upstairs," she said, standing.

Kaleb put away the chair. "Good night."

Rylee grinned. "I'm not going to bed just yet. I'll be up for a while. I'm just going to do some reading."

He watched her ascend the stairs. The massage had been a mistake on his part. Kaleb was going to have a hard time forgetting how silky smooth her neck and shoulders felt beneath his fingers.

He'd managed to ease her stress, but it wasn't going to be that easy to rid himself of the tension in his own body.

Chapter Ten

Rylee's skin still prickled from Kaleb's touch. His closeness had been so male, so bracing, sending shivers of delight through her.

She liked him. More than she cared to admit. She didn't like that he thought of her as a victim, because she wasn't one. And she didn't need his protection. She was more than capable of protecting herself. She just needed his help. Once she was back in California, they would go their separate ways.

She couldn't wait to go home. She yearned to see her mother and her friends again.

She thought of Calderon. He was responsible for the chaos she found herself in, and she vowed to make him pay. She was ready to march into battle against this criminal who was behind Stuart's murder and the attempt on her life. But she needed solid evidence against him.

He was smart. But being smart couldn't keep Calderon from making a mistake. He'd made a costly one by leaving her alive.

She stared out the window from the guest bedroom, admiring the moonlight dancing on the lake. She looked up and sighed.

Rylee walked away from the window, a tear rolling down her cheek.

She crawled into bed, sitting on top of the covers.

After Kaleb's massage, Rylee felt completely relaxed and only meant to close her eyes for a few minutes.

She woke up an hour later.

Rylee sat up in bed, using the pillows to support her back. There was a knock at her door.

"Yes…"

"It's me."

"C'mon in, Kaleb," Rylee said.

He opened the door. "I wanted to check on you."

She smiled. "I'm fine."

"Are you really okay?" he asked from the doorway. "You've been thrown back into the same chaos all over again. I'm so sorry, Rylee."

"It's not your fault. You didn't even know I existed until that night. I hate that you and Nate are now caught up in this."

"I told you—we're good. And I won't fight you on going to Los Angeles."

His words thrilled her. Rylee resisted the urge to jump out of bed and throw her arms around him. "Kaleb, thank you. You've made my night. My mother's birthday is in two weeks. I really want to be there to celebrate with her, but I can't risk her safety."

He met her gaze. "Before you get too happy, I can't promise you'll be home by your mother's birthday. We'll take it on a day-by-day basis."

"That's fair."

Kaleb gave a slight nod. "Well, I'll let you get some rest. See you in the morning."

"Thanks again," Rylee said.

When he left, she tossed off the covers, got out of bed and did a little dance. *I'm going home. Oh, Mama… I can't wait to see you.*

An image of Calderon appeared in her mind. *I'm taking you down.*

BRENDA WAS WAITING for Kaleb inside Carol's Martini Bar.

Her thick, dark hair hung in long graceful curls over her shoulders. Her face was a perfect oval with striking eyes and full lips.

She embraced him as if they'd known each other for years.

Brenda grinned. "It's good to see you again. I'm thrilled you were able to meet me for drinks."

He stepped out of her hug. "It's my pleasure."

They found an empty table for two and sat down.

Brenda flipped her hair over her shoulders. "How is your day going?"

"Fine so far," Kaleb responded.

A waitress came to the table to take their drink orders.

"I'll have a dirty martini," she told the server.

"Beer on tap," he stated.

When the waitress walked away, Kaleb asked, "How was your day?"

"It was okay. It's still a bit strange not seeing Easton at his desk. I think Nova had a moment this morning when she got to work."

He nodded. "She and her father were very close."

"I know," Brenda murmured. "I loved seeing the two of them together."

His eyes came up to study her face. "You look troubled."

"Well…the truth is, I'm a little concerned about something I heard at work today," she responded. "I heard that there might be a leak in our office. They believe that's what got Easton killed."

He studied her expression. "What do you think?"

Brenda shrugged. "I have no idea. Right now, I just don't know what to think."

"I'm sure they will figure it out. I may not be a marshal anymore, but there are still some great ones in that office."

"I feel the same way," she responded. "It's just that I'm beginning to sense the tension in the office."

The waitress returned with their drinks.

Brenda took a sip of her dirty martini, then said, "So, you're now in private security. I bet that's exciting."

"Not really," Kaleb responded. "I'm more of a glorified bodyguard to high-profile clients."

"Like celebrities?"

"A few."

"Anyone you can tell me about?" Brenda asked.

Kaleb shook his head no. "I'm afraid not."

They sat in silence for a moment before she asked, "How well do you know Nova?"

"I've known her about as long as I've known her parents. Why do you ask?"

"She's really sweet. I've been worried about her since Easton's death. Then witnessing her breakdown at work this morning... I feel bad for her."

Kaleb's heart sank as she spoke. Although he was feeling the pain of grief, it could not compare to the sorrow of a daughter losing her parent. "It's hard to go through something like that."

"I know firsthand about that kind of grief," Brenda said. "I lost both my parents at a very young age."

"I'm sorry."

"It's fine," she said. "It took me a while to get over it, but I finally did. Have you and Nova dated?"

"No..." He wondered at her line of questioning. "Where did that come from?"

"I was just curious. I hope I didn't upset you..."

"You didn't," Kaleb said. He took a swig of his beer, then said, "At the funeral, there were quite a few faces I didn't recognize. The only person I remember is John Martin... I'm a bit surprised to see how he's come up financially. Certainly looks like he hit the lottery or something."

"All I know is that John and his wife suddenly started spending money like it was going out of style. They travel to the West Coast at least once a month, and they just got back from Morocco. I even heard that they're building a house in Costa Rica."

He kept his tone casual as he said, "From the looks of it, he can certainly afford it."

Brenda nodded. "When I first came to work with the marshals three years ago, he was just a regular guy. I've heard different stories about how he got his money. You know how the rumor mill goes…"

She continued to jabber on about other office rumors. Brenda was willing to talk, but he wondered if she really knew anything that could help him find the leak.

"Anyway, enough about work," she said. "I'd like to know what you do for fun."

"I work out and play ball," Kaleb responded. "It relaxes me. What about you?"

"I love to travel. Every year I try to experience new places. This summer I'm going to Tokyo. Have you ever been there?"

"A long time ago," he responded. "I was stationed at the marine base in Iwakuni, about six hundred miles from Tokyo."

"You'll have to give me some pointers on what to see or where to go."

"I'm sure things have changed quite a bit since I was there."

Brenda ordered a second dirty martini. "Kaleb, I'm going to be honest with you. I find you extremely attractive and this air of mystery all around you—it's so sexy." Her eyes never left his gaze as she stuck an olive in her mouth. "I invited you here in hopes that we could get to know each other better."

He raised an eyebrow.

She laughed. "Is that too direct for you?"

Kaleb shook his head. "I just didn't expect that to come out of your mouth."

"What did you think I was going to say?"

"You didn't strike me as the assertive type."

"So, you thought I was passive?"

"Not at all. You just seemed sweet, almost a bit nervous." Kaleb assumed this because of the way she'd rambled on in the beginning. She seemed much more relaxed now. He wondered if the martini had put her more at ease.

"I was nervous initially," Brenda admitted. "I know this isn't a date or anything, but you're the first guy I've been in a public setting like this with in a couple of months. I moved here with my ex, but then things changed between us when we got to Milwaukee. I ended things about six months ago. After a few nightmarish dates, I just gave up."

"I find that hard to believe," he responded. "You're a beautiful woman, Brenda."

"Thank you for saying that." She took a sip of her drink. "I have to ask…are you in a relationship—or worse…married? I guess I should've led with this question."

Kaleb chuckled. "I'm not involved with anyone. I wouldn't be here if I were."

Brenda released an audible sigh of relief. "Thank goodness!"

He wasn't interested in pursuing anything with her and didn't want to lead her on. "My immediate focus is on building up my company's reputation, finding the right employees and maintaining client relations."

"Is that your way of saying that you're too busy for a relationship?" she asked.

"I suppose it is," Kaleb admitted. "I don't want to play with your heart."

"I appreciate that," Brenda responded. "So, to be clear… are you saying you're not interested in me?"

"I'm happy to meet with you, but I have to be honest. My real focus is finding out who killed Easton."

Brenda smiled. "I guess this means that we won't be ending this evening back at my place or yours."

"No, we're not," Kaleb responded. "I know I advised you against talking about agency business, but I really need your help. If you hear anything that could help, please give me a call."

"Of course. I don't mind helping you since you used to work for the agency. Especially if it's for Easton."

He smiled. "Thank you."

Brenda offered up a grin once more. "You know…we can at least extend this to dinner."

"Maybe another time," he responded. "I have some work to do this evening."

"Another time then," she murmured.

"I'd like that," Kaleb said as he paid the check.

They left the bar.

He walked Brenda to her car before heading to his own.

"This was not exactly how I saw this evening ending," she said. "But I've really enjoyed your company, Kaleb."

"Same here," he responded. "Have a good night."

"Kaleb…what do you think happened with the witness he was protecting?" Brenda asked.

"I don't know," he said, keeping his expression blank.

Chapter Eleven

Rylee glanced at the clock on the wall with rising dismay.

Kaleb had been gone for well over an hour and a half. She felt frustrated over his freedom to come and go as he pleased. She wasn't allowed to leave the house, and she was going a little stir-crazy because of it.

Rylee seriously doubted Brenda would be able to tell Kaleb much. But then again, she might be able to offer valuable insight into John Martin.

If their suspicions about the agent proved correct, John just might be connected to Calderon. She wanted Calderon behind bars in the worst way. She reviewed her notes on the man. A former lieutenant who was willing to testify against Raul Mancuso a few years ago had said that the drug leader paid Calderon a million dollars a year in salary. He'd said Calderon and Raul were close. They traveled almost everywhere together using fake credentials, including a fake US visa. Unfortunately, the witness had died of a heart attack before he could testify.

She laid the iPad beside her.

Her gaze strayed back to the clock as she wondered how things were going between Kaleb and Brenda.

"It's not my business," she whispered.

She heard footsteps behind her and glanced over her

shoulder. "Nate…hey." She hadn't seen him until now. Rylee just assumed he'd been in his office working all day.

"Kaleb's not back yet?"

"No," she responded. "Maybe drinks turned into dinner."

"I doubt that," Nate stated. "I know my brother. He's not staying out any longer than he has to—your safety is his priority."

"He doesn't have to worry about me. I can take care of myself, and you're here," Rylee responded. "I'm fine."

"Why don't we get something to eat?" Nate suggested. "You can pick the restaurant and we'll have it delivered."

"Sounds good to me."

He grabbed some menus from a drawer in the kitchen. Nate handed them to Rylee.

"I'm in the mood for Italian," she said.

He grinned. "Me, too."

KALEB TEXTED HIS brother before leaving the bar's parking lot.

Stopping by my place first to grab some clothes. Be there soon.

Just as he pulled out onto the street, his phone rang.

"Hello…"

"Kaleb, I'm scared," Brenda said. "I think I'm being followed."

He checked his rearview mirror to see if he had a tail. "What makes you think that?"

"This black car has been behind me since I left the bar. It may be nothing, but I've never noticed any car staying behind me all the way home. I'm a block from my house and I'm afraid to stop."

"Don't. Just drive straight to the police station," Kaleb instructed. "Then ping me your location."

"Okay."

Kaleb could hear the fear in her voice. He didn't doubt she was telling the truth, but what he couldn't figure out was why someone would be following her.

Brenda sent her location, and he headed in that direction.

When Kaleb arrived, he found her sitting inside the station, looking frightened. She was trembling.

"Were you followed here to the station?" he asked.

Brenda nodded. "Yes. I think the car even circled back around."

"What did it look like?"

"It was a black Mercedes sedan. I'm not sure of the exact model."

"Anything else you noticed?"

"I…" She paused. "I think John Martin drives one like it."

"John has a Maserati."

"He owns several cars," she said. "He normally drives a BMW SUV to work, but I've seen him in a black Mercedes a few times."

"You should call the agency and update them. They'll make sure you get home safely."

She took his hand in her own. "Can't *you* stay here with me?"

"I can't. I have work to do." Kaleb glanced outside. "You should be safe here. I don't see the car you mentioned anywhere."

"Thank you for coming."

"By any chance, do you think it was John who tailed you?"

Brenda shook her head. "No… I see him at work, but we don't really talk. He mostly keeps to himself. I can't think of a reason why he'd be following me."

"Okay," he responded. "Well, let me know when you make it home."

She gave him a tiny smile. "I will."

Kaleb left the station and got back into his truck. He sat there for a while, looking around. He didn't see the car Brenda described anywhere. Maybe it was her imagination. She could've wrongly assumed someone was following her. It was up to the police and marshals' service to sort it out— he wanted to get back to Rylee.

But first he had a stop to make.

KALEB NOTICED A black Mercedes parked down the street from his house. If Brenda had indeed been followed, then he had a feeling this was the same vehicle. From where he was, Kaleb couldn't get a clear view of the driver—he wasn't sure whether someone was sitting in the car or not.

Erring on the side of caution, Kaleb decided to go with the theory that whoever had followed Brenda also knew where he lived, proving that there was definitely a breach within the agency.

He debated whether to confront the driver but decided against it. Why was Brenda followed? She must have said something to someone in the office about meeting him for drinks. Maybe they thought Kaleb would end up at her place. When she went to the police station, they'd decided to come to his house.

Kaleb could feel the stifling presence of a watcher as he slowly unlocked his door. He took a deep breath before entering, retreating into the safety of his home and flicking on the lights. Every creak from the floorboards sent chills along his spine as he made his way upstairs to his bedroom.

Inside the closet, Kaleb reached for a small suitcase. He needed to grab some more clothes. A sound from behind had him spinning. He was not alone. A figure stood in his bed-room, back to Kaleb. Someone had sneaked into the house.

Kaleb's heart pounded in his chest like a relentless drum as he watched the menacing stranger through the narrow slit of the closet door. The intruder, a formidable figure with a buzz cut, burly muscles and a thick beard, cast an ominous shadow in his leather jacket and boots. His predatory gaze swept across the room, searching, relentless. Time was of the essence, and Kaleb knew he had to act swiftly.

With nerves of steel, he emerged from the concealment of the closet, his voice edged with determination. "Who are you?" he demanded.

The stranger pivoted, a malevolent sneer distorting his features. "None of your business," he spat with defiance.

"I'm going to give you a chance to walk out of my house."

A chilling chuckle escaped the intruder's lips. "I don't think so," he retorted, drawing nearer. "I'm looking for some-one, and you know who it is. You can make a lot of money if you tell me what I want to know."

"I don't know who you're talking about, and I don't need your money." Kaleb maintained his resolute stance.

The stranger's eyes narrowed, the threat now palpable. "You're lying," he growled, advancing menacingly. "You know something. I guess I'll have to find out for myself," he declared, reaching into his jacket.

Before the intruder could retrieve whatever concealed weapon lay within, Kaleb had his gun drawn, its barrel un-wavering. "I think it's time you leave."

"Mister, you don't want to do this…" the stranger began, but Kaleb's resolve was unwavering.

"You can walk out of here now or be carried out."

In an abrupt surge of motion, the intruder kicked the gun

out of his hand. The enforcer propelled himself forward, his imposing physique charging with unstoppable force.

Kaleb's fists were a relentless flurry of blows, an on-slaught aimed at overpowering his opponent. The adversary, however, displayed remarkable agility. Their intricate interplay of evasion and aggression unfolded like a brutal dance, a fierce exchange of strikes and defensive maneuvers.

Kaleb reclaimed his weapon and pointed it at the enforcer. He observed the man's internal turmoil, his eyes flickering with indecision. A seasoned judge of character, he sensed desperation and danger emanating from the intruder.

"Whoever you're looking for is not worth dying for," he said. "Get out of my house, and I better not see you around here again."

Defeated, the stranger sighed, his surrender evident. Slowly, he retreated, hands raised in defeat.

Kaleb kept his gun trained on the man until he clambered into his parked vehicle across the street and sped away, leaving Kaleb with the echoes of averted violence reverberating in the room.

He exhaled, the tension in his body dissipating. He holstered his gun and looked outside before grabbing a few clothing items from his bedroom.

He left through the front door and called Nate from an untraceable phone.

"Hey, I got held up." He quickly recapped what happened earlier. "I had a visitor. He left when I pulled my weapon. I'm on the way to your place. It may take me a minute, because I want to make sure I'm not being followed."

"Did you get a glimpse of the license plate?"

"Naw, but according to Brenda, John Martin owns a Mercedes just like the one she saw following her. Then the same model vehicle was parked over my way, only it was driven by a dude with a buzz cut and beard."

"Interesting. You still think John is the leak?"

"It could just be a coincidence, but I think he's connected somehow to what happened," Kaleb responded. "What are the chances of Brenda being followed and that same car parking near my house?"

"But why follow her in the first place? If they knew where you lived, then why not just follow you, Kaleb?"

"Maybe they wanted to scare Brenda," he suggested.

"So, let's go with that theory," Nate said. "Maybe they went to your place to see if she was with you."

"I'm beginning to think Brenda may be a target. But *why*?"

"They must believe she knows something, even if Brenda doesn't realize it."

"You might be right," Kaleb said. He trusted the marshals would keep her safe. He was confident that Brenda would keep him updated. He was hyperfocused on keeping his promise to Easton and Rylee.

"How's Rylee holding up?" Kaleb asked.

"Bored," Nate said. "I just saw her head to the workout room. Hopefully, she'll burn off some of that frustration."

It bothered Kaleb to catch glimpses of sadness in her eyes. Rylee wanted to be reunited with her mother. He wanted to make her wish come true. But he couldn't forget that someone wanted to kill her.

RYLEE WAS IN the middle of her stretches when Kaleb entered the workout room.

"Hey, how was your *date*?" she asked, not looking at him. She didn't want him seeing her relief at his return.

He laughed. "It was just drinks and conversation. Nothing more."

She gave him a sidelong glance.

Kaleb sat down on a bench near the door. "When I left the bar, Brenda called me saying that someone followed her after she left."

Rylee stopped stretching. "Really?"

He nodded. "She sounded terrified. I told her to go to the police station and wait until someone from her office arrived to make sure she got home safely. But when I got to my house, the same car she described was parked across the street. Brenda may be in danger if they think she knows anything."

"Does she know anything?" Rylee asked, reaching for her towel.

"Not that I could tell."

Patting her neck, she said, "If we want to pin down the leak and our focus is Martin, we'd have to prove his money came from the cartel. We need to follow it and the source. We also need to see if the money that was found in Stuart's account came from the same place."

"This won't clear your partner's name," Kaleb warned.

"No, but it helps me figure out where to go next," Rylee replied with a slight edge to her voice. An edge of determination. He took a step closer, and despite herself, she felt the familiar pull toward him that she had tried so hard to deny. It was becoming harder for her to ignore the way her heart raced in his presence. If only she could have a normal life— one free from danger and fear.

Rylee focused on the task at hand, trying to suppress her feelings for Kaleb. She knew that getting involved with him would only complicate things. She took a deep breath and continued, "I need to find the real culprit who framed my partner. I won't rest until I find them."

Kaleb nodded. "We'll work together to clear your partner's name."

Rylee felt a wave of gratitude wash over her. She trusted him more than anyone else.

ONCE AGAIN, Kaleb was struck by Rylee's beauty. Her classic features and high cheekbones accentuated the slenderness of her face and her perfectly shaped nose. She had a mouth he found incredibly sexy. Her easy smile lit up the room. For just a moment, as he gazed at Rylee, he saw a hint of vulnerability in the depths of her eyes, and a renewed surge of protectiveness welled up inside him.

He gave himself a mental shake. She obviously could handle herself. Still, he was going to honor his commitment to Easton.

The truth was that since he'd left the marshals' service, Kaleb's heart had been filled with the darkness of loss and shame. Even now, he wasn't quite ready to leave that blackness behind. It motivated him to keep his clients safe.

Kaleb reminded himself that no matter how attracted he was to Rylee, she was a fascination he didn't need to explore.

It was almost eleven when Kaleb headed upstairs.

Rylee walked out of the guest room dressed in a pair of navy blue fleece jogging pants and a white-and-navy T-shirt. She wore a pair of thick navy socks.

"I thought you'd be asleep."

"Not yet," Rylee replied. "I have too much on my mind. One of which is that I need to get out of this house. I need to maintain some kind of normal life."

Kaleb could see the longing in her eyes for the outdoors as she watched the trees sway through the window. "We can take a walk around the neighborhood. It's not a good idea to wander around as if you don't have a target on your back, Rylee."

"Thank you, Kaleb. I just need to feel some fresh air on my face." She swallowed hard, then said, "I know you'll be as happy as I will when this is over. I'll have my life back, and you can return to yours."

He nodded, resigned to her response. She was returning to Los Angeles, and his life was in Milwaukee. They just weren't meant to be.

Chapter Twelve

Rylee felt a spark of excitement at the prospect of being out-doors, despite the freezing cold that nipped at her. She couldn't wait to inhale the crisp, refreshing air. Swiftly, she dressed in thermal underwear, jeans and a cozy sweatshirt. With deft fingers, she fluffed up her dark curls in front of the mirror, her reflection capturing her final scrutiny before she left the bedroom and made her way downstairs.

"I'm making dinner," she announced when she entered the kitchen.

Nate glanced at her. "Hey…you won't get an argument out of me."

"What's going on?" Kaleb inquired as he joined them.

Nate said, "Rylee's making dinner for us."

Kaleb flashed a smile at Rylee, and a warm sensation settled in the pit of her stomach. "Thank you."

"You might not want to thank me just yet," she teased. "I'm going to try something new."

After the meal was prepared, they gathered around the table to indulge in homemade waffles, fried chicken wings, and slices of avocado and tomato.

"Everything is delicious," Nate complimented.

"Cooking actually relaxes me," Rylee revealed. "Besides, it's the least I can do for the two of you. I can make chicken enchiladas tomorrow night if you can pick up a few things from the store."

Kaleb's eyes lit up. "Did Nate tell you that I love Mexican food?"

"No, he didn't. I must confess it was mostly a selfish thought," she admitted with a playful grin. "It's what I was craving."

Laughter filled the room, a welcome respite from their circumstances.

Kaleb exuded an energy that seemed to pulse in the atmosphere around them, drawing Rylee in. Perhaps it was because she'd been in isolation for the past fifteen months, which made him strike a vibrant chord deep within her. His broad shoulders seemed like they could bear the weight of the world.

"One more thing… I need a cell phone," she said.

"That's not a problem—we can get you a new one," Kaleb assured her.

"Thanks." Rylee skewered a piece of avocado with her fork.

After dinner, she cleared the table, then made preparations for her outing.

Dressed in a puffy, fleece-lined black jacket, a black knit cap and a matching scarf wrapped snugly around her neck, Rylee entered the living room.

Kaleb joined her a few minutes later. "Ready?"

"I am," Rylee responded with a smile.

They stepped outside.

"This place is truly beautiful," she remarked. "But I'm sure you've already figured out that I have a real love-hate relationship with cold weather."

"LA is nice," Kaleb agreed. "I've been out there a few times. The traffic is intense, but I enjoyed the city."

"I can't wait to go home. I miss my mom terribly. I want to call her, but I don't want to put her in any danger."

"I know that this has been really hard on you."

"More than you know. She's more than just my mother; she's also my best friend."

Kaleb nodded in understanding. "I feel the same way about my mom." He glanced at her. "We're going to get you back there, Rylee. I give my word."

"Thank you. The other thing I miss is my job. I loved being with Homeland Security."

"I looked into working with them at one point," Kaleb shared. "But eventually decided to go with the marshals."

Rylee was having a good time, enjoying Kaleb's company. Yet, she continued to fight her growing feelings for him. There was no time to focus on a relationship until she was no longer on the run. She didn't want to bring anyone else into this chaos, even though Kaleb was already deeply involved.

"This is a perfect place to visit from time to time in the summer. I'm not a big fan of fishing, but I like the town," she said.

"The temperature gets up to eighty degrees," Kaleb informed her.

"I need it a bit warmer, I'm afraid," she replied with a chuckle.

"So, you like a-hundred-degree weather?"

"It doesn't bother me," Rylee stated. "I'm used to temperatures like that."

"I get it. I don't mind the cold, having grown up in Milwaukee."

She nodded. "I really appreciate everything you and Nate have done to keep me safe," Rylee expressed her gratitude.

"I'm glad to be able to help," Kaleb responded.

"Seriously. I don't know if I'd have made it without you."

"Easton called me that night because he knew I'd come to his aid. I only wish I could've gotten there earlier."

"He knew you were coming," Rylee explained. "That's why he sent me to the panic room. He told me not to come out. I tried to convince him to come with me, but he wouldn't hear of it."

"I'm surprised you didn't try to shoot your way out."

"Actually, that was my plan," she admitted. "But Easton... I don't know why he wouldn't just come with me."

"I wish I had an answer for you," Kaleb said. "I wondered the same thing. Knowing him as well as I do, I'm sure Easton's primary focus was protecting you. Maybe he thought if they didn't find you, they wouldn't keep looking in Wisconsin."

Kaleb wasn't the only one keeping an eye on the neighborhood. Rylee remained vigilant. She understood that she was not out of danger yet, but for now, she wanted to relish the moment.

"I needed this, but I'm cold now. I need to thaw out."

Kaleb's cell phone rang minutes after they reentered the house.

He checked the caller ID. "I need to take this."

"I bet that's Brenda," Rylee whispered to Nate.

He nodded in agreement.

"If your brother isn't careful, he might find himself a wife."

"You just might be right about that," Nate responded with a chuckle.

THE NEXT DAY during dinner, Rylee said, "I've been trying to figure out a way to get evidence to take down Calderon."

"You're the only witness alive who can implicate him in a murder. His mission is to eliminate anyone he considers a threat."

"Yeah, I know. That's why I'm so frustrated. If it's the last thing I do, I'm taking him down."

"If you try to do this alone, it just may be the last thing you do."

"I'm aware of that," Ryle responded tersely.

"You have to know I'm on your side," Kaleb said.

Rylee narrowed her eyes as she settled back in her chair. "Kaleb, I've spent most of my adult life trying to protect this country. I became an HSI agent to fight the war against drugs. I know it's a dangerous job, but I can handle it."

"These enchiladas are delicious," Nate interjected.

She glanced over at him and smiled. "I'm glad you like them."

Some of the tension in the air evaporated. Rylee realized she was overreacting. She took a moment to reclaim her peace.

"My brother's right," Kaleb said. "The food is on point."

Rylee pasted on a smile. "Thanks."

After dinner, she went to the workout room. Kaleb was in there lifting weights.

"I didn't mean to be so argumentative earlier," Rylee said. "It's just that I'm still a special agent—at least in my head. I do know the risks. I know people can die. I almost did… Kaleb, I'm highly trained."

He set the weights down beside him. "I guess I see you as my client. I never met you as HSI Special Agent Green."

"I didn't meet you as a US marshal, but I trust you to keep me safe."

"I see your point. My apologies, Rylee."

"We have to trust each other, and this has to be a team effort," she stated.

"I agree," he responded. He gestured toward the equipment. "Do you want to join me?"

"Sure."

Rylee got on the treadmill while he resumed working with

the weights. She hoped exercising would help clear her mind. The last thing she wanted was to be at odds with Kaleb. She only wished he trusted her more.

KALEB REGRETTED ASKING Rylee to work out with him. He was having a hard time staying focused. He finally abandoned the weights.

He sat there for a moment watching Rylee.

Kaleb wanted to kiss her. He'd wanted to kiss her so badly, it still burned in his bones almost an hour later. That night, it had taken a while for him to finally fall asleep because he couldn't get her out of his mind.

And when he woke up the next morning, Kaleb still wanted to kiss her.

He pulled himself out of bed before 6:00 a.m., showered, dressed and navigated to the office. He wanted to follow up with a couple of potential clients who'd inquired about their services.

He was interested in Rylee like he'd never been attracted to a woman. Kaleb searched inside his heart, wondering if his fascination with her was because she shared his love for this country and wanting to right the injustices of this world.

Spending time with Rylee in such close quarters, he'd come to admire her strength, courage and determination.

His phone began vibrating.

Kaleb sprinted out of the office, barely catching his phone on the fourth ring.

"Hello?"

"This is John Martin."

"John...hi," Kaleb said into the phone, his body tense with anticipation.

"It's about Easton and his missing witness... I need to talk to you. Can you meet me at the Grand Avenue Mall around seven o'clock? Near the food court."

He was curious to hear what John had to say. "Sure. I'll see you at seven." John was suspicious, but there was something in his voice... He sounded afraid. Had the man who Kaleb thought was the leak found the actual leak?

John hung up.

Kaleb stood in the doorway, facing Rylee. "Come with me."

They walked into Nate's office.

"John just called me," he announced. "He wants to meet."

Rylee and Nate exchanged surprised looks.

"He says it's about Easton and you, Rylee."

"I don't think you should meet him alone," she said. "I'll go with you."

He shook his head no. "You can't be seen. Nate can come along for backup."

"You're not leaving me here," she said. "I'm going with y'all."

There was little doubt that Rylee was upset. He could tell by the way she glared at him, but Kaleb was adamant about his decision. "I can't risk your safety or have John discover that you've been with me this entire time. He's still a marshal."

"I guess I see your point," Rylee mumbled.

Kaleb sighed, knowing how frustrated she must be. "John wants to meet at the Grand Avenue Mall near the food court."

"That's probably a good idea," Nate said. "I can easily merge with the other people in the area."

"At least let me stay in Nate's car," Rylee stated. "Nobody will be able to see me with those dark windows."

Kaleb released a soft sigh of resignation. He should've known better than to expect her to willingly stay where she was safe. "Fine, but you *have* to stay in the car, Rylee."

"I will," she responded.

He met her eyes. "I mean it."

"I give you my word." Her tone was strong and resolute.

A few minutes past six, they prepared to drive to Milwaukee. Fifty minutes later, Kaleb got out of the car, walked to the designated location and waited.

He glimpsed Nate standing a few yards away, bundled up in a coat, scarf and knit cap.

Underneath his coat, Kaleb wore a bulletproof vest. He wasn't sure he could trust John at this point, so it was best to be careful.

Another hour passed, and no sign of John.

Kaleb checked his phone. No calls or messages.

He decided to wait another thirty minutes. He stole a peek at his brother, then gave a slight shrug.

When there was still no sign of John, he decided the trip had been a waste of time. Keenly aware of his surroundings, Kaleb headed back to the car.

Nate followed at a distance.

Back in Whitefish Bay, they went into the house and settled down in the family room.

"What just happened?" Rylee asked. "Nate told me that John never showed up."

"I have no idea," Kaleb responded.

Rylee looked confused. "Why would he go to all this trouble? It just doesn't make sense."

"I agree," Nate said. "Maybe he got held up with work."

"I'm not interested in playing this game," Kaleb stated. He felt frustrated because he had no optimism—no real expectation that they were getting any closer to discovering the identity of the person responsible for Easton's death. "I tried calling John several times during the drive back here. It went to voice mail each time."

"This doesn't add up," Nate said. "He reached out to *you*."

"If I don't hear from him by tomorrow, I'm going to his house."

Nate's phone rang.

"I need to take this," he said before heading to his office.

Fifteen minutes passed before he reappeared, his voice laced with excitement and urgency. "I've got it," he exclaimed, his eyes filled with an intense determination. "I just got off the phone with a friend—he's a forensic accountant. We found the source of John's money. It's a combination of factors. His wife's grandmother left her a substantial inheritance, and John's been making astute investments. His portfolio is truly impressive."

"He could still be the leak," Rylee said. "Maybe he was hoping I'd be with you."

"That's why I didn't want you to come along," Kaleb told her. "However, I don't think it's John. It was something in his voice… I believe he found the leak."

"So why not show up for the meeting that *he* set up?" she asked.

"I don't know," Kaleb said, "but I intend to find out."

Chapter Thirteen

"I know why John Martin didn't show up last night," Nate announced the next morning when he joined Kaleb and Rylee for breakfast. "He's dead."

Rylee dropped her fork, her heart pounding erratically. "What do you mean, he's *dead*?" She bit her lip until it throbbed like her pulse.

"Last night...his wife came home from an event and found his body. Apparently, someone broke in and shot him."

"And they're sure that it wasn't a suicide?" Kaleb questioned.

Shaking his head, Nate responded, "No, he was murdered. I just got off the phone with Nova. She said she tried calling you not too long ago."

Kaleb scrubbed a hand down his face. "I must have been in the shower. I haven't even looked at my cell yet. We now have two dead marshals and no solid leads."

"It was probably the guy who came after me," Rylee stated in a low, tormented voice. "Something just doesn't seem right about this. My gut tells me that John knew he could trust you and that's why he contacted you. Someone killed him before he could get to you. I have a feeling ballistics will show that John and Easton were killed by the same gun."

Kaleb looked at his brother. "Why don't we hack into his security system? At least Rylee will be able to identify the shooter if it is this Luis person."

"I already thought about that," Nate said. "There's no footage because it was off-line for some reason. The police couldn't get anything, either."

"We know John wouldn't have disconnected it," Rylee said. "So it had to be the person who shot him."

Kaleb and Nate agreed, and they finished their breakfast in silence.

"Listen, we haven't lost this battle yet," Kaleb said.

"We haven't won any victories, either," Rylee said. Swallowing the sob in her throat, she looked up at him and said, "People are dying because of me."

"Rylee..."

"No, Easton and John are both dead, and it's my fault. I don't want anything to happen to you and your brother. I think it's best if I leave."

"I don't agree," Kaleb said. "Knowing John the way I do, he probably confronted the person he suspected, and that's what got him killed."

Despite what Kaleb said, Rylee knew what she had to do.

WHILE KALEB WAS in the office with Nate, Rylee grabbed her backpack and left the house. She wasn't going to let anyone else die on her behalf.

I never should've called Easton that night. I should have just driven straight out of town.

She walked a few blocks to a shopping center, relishing the feeling of walking freely outside, then scheduled an Uber on the phone Nate had given her yesterday.

Rylee waited inside the corner market for her ride to show up.

When her transportation arrived, she got in quickly. "I need you to take me to a car dealership."

Rylee glanced over her shoulder to see if there was any sign of Kaleb or Nate.

I'm protecting them by leaving. They don't need to be caught up in this.

After a short distance, the Uber dropped Rylee off in front of a small car lot.

She walked around, looking at the different vehicles for sale. Her plan was to buy a car and leave town. She was going to Los Angeles.

An eager salesman walked her way, grinning.

"I'm just looking right now," Rylee said as she walked over to a Ford SUV. "I'll let you know if I find anything."

"Are you looking for anything particular?"

"Not really. This is kind of spur-of-the-moment."

"I'll be right over there if you need me."

She smiled and nodded.

Rylee walked over to a used Honda Accord and peered inside. Her first car had been a Honda, and she'd loved it.

She checked out a few more vehicles, but her mind kept returning to the Honda. It was going to take most of her savings. She had enough in her checking account to get her to California. However, it wouldn't leave much of a cushion if she had mechanical issues along the way.

Maybe I should just rent a car.

Rylee walked back over to the Honda. Since it would be a cash purchase, she could negotiate some on the price. Soon she'd be on the road. Heading to LA to find answers, to get her life back…and to take down the man who'd stolen it.

"WHERE'S RYLEE?" Nate asked from the doorway of the office, where Kaleb was working on a contract for a new client.

"She's upstairs."

"No, she's not. I was just up there."

Kaleb pushed away from the desk and got up. "Did you check the workout room?"

He nodded. "She's not there, either. I think she's gone. Her suitcase is still here, but not the backpack."

Kaleb sighed in frustration. "Rylee's going to get herself killed…"

"I can track her phone," Nate said, navigating to the desk. "Hopefully, she hasn't gotten rid of it. Why do you think she left? Did something happen between you two?"

"We didn't get into a fight, if that's what you're thinking," he responded. "She was upset the last time I spoke to her. She's blaming herself for the deaths of Easton and John."

Nate sat down in front of the computer.

Pacing, Kaleb said, "I hope she hasn't gotten too far."

"We'll find her if she still has the phone you gave her with her."

"That woman…"

"Kaleb, it's all right," Nate stated while scanning the monitor. "She hasn't gone too far. Looks like Rylee's looking for a car. She's at a used car dealership. The one on Bay Street."

"I'm headed there now. Let me know if she leaves."

"Will do."

He rushed to the car and got in.

Rylee, what are you doing? Are you trying to get yourself killed?

Kaleb ignored his racing heart. He was so focused on finding her, he almost ran a red light.

Keep it together.

His fingers clasped tightly around the steering wheel, Kaleb inhaled deeply, then released the breath slowly as he tried to will the next light to change to green. He had no idea when Rylee had left the house. *I have to find her. I'm not going to let another person die on my watch.*

Kaleb pulled into the used car lot and parked in front. He got out, searching for her. He found her looking at a Honda and walked briskly toward her.

Rylee's back was to him, so she didn't know he was there.

"If you wanted to go car shopping, all you had to do was ask."

She straightened, then turned around to face him. "How did you find me?"

Kaleb didn't respond.

"Your brother tracked the phone he gave me," she stated, realization dawning.

"Rylee, what's going on with you? I thought we had an understanding."

"It should be obvious to you—I don't want you or Nate to get hurt, or worse. I figured it was best to put some distance between us."

"Nobody knows you're with me."

"If John figured it out, then someone else will."

"John never mentioned that. He just said he had something to tell me about Easton and his witness. That was it."

"Just let me go," she said. "This isn't your problem."

He shook his head no. "We're a team. I made a promise to Easton that I'd keep you safe, and I mean to do just that."

There was a pensive shimmer in the shadow of her eyes. "You're the one who's been telling me just what a dangerous person Calderon is and I should stay away from him—maybe you should take your own advice."

"There's strength in numbers."

"Two innocent people are dead, Kaleb."

"Come back to the house. We can talk about all this when we get there."

She gave a reluctant nod, then followed him to the car.

"I'm not going to apologize for leaving," she said.

"I didn't expect you would."

He left the parking lot and merged into the traffic.

"Rylee, you can't just take off like that. I know how much you want to go home, but you have to put your emotions aside. Did you consider what might happen if you broke down somewhere on the road alone? And where would you stay? People are looking for Rylee Greenwood."

"I thought about all those things, Kaleb," she responded. "I did."

"And you still decided to run."

"I thought it would keep you and Nate safe."

Kaleb reached over and took her hand in his own. "Rylee, it's my job to keep *you* safe."

His phone rang.

She eyed him.

"It's Brenda," he stated.

"You should take it," she responded, moving her hand out of his reach. "I'm curious as to what she has to say about John's death."

"Me, too, but it will have to wait until we get back to the house."

She nodded in understanding.

"I hope you won't run off again," he said. "I don't want anything to happen to you."

"I won't," she responded, then stared out the window.

"I'll be upstairs," Rylee said when they returned to the house. "And you don't have to worry. I'm not going anywhere."

"Is she okay?" Nate asked as Kaleb entered the kitchen.

"Yeah. Rylee thought we'd be safe if she wasn't around."

"Where is she?"

"In the guest room."

Alone in the office, Kaleb pulled up his call list and clicked on Brenda's name.

She answered on the first ring, saying, "I have some distressing news. I don't know if you've heard, but John Martin is dead. Someone *killed* him."

Brenda sounded as if she'd been crying.

"I heard. It was on the news this morning."

"John and I were friendly, but we weren't what you'd call friends. We just worked in the same office." She paused a moment, then said, "I can't believe this."

"Unfortunately, things like this happen."

"I know, but we're still processing Easton's death. Now John... There's just been some strange things happening."

"Like what?" Kaleb asked.

"Well, Easton's death, his missing witness, my being followed and now John's dead, too. I can't help but wonder if they're all connected."

"You haven't been followed since, have you?"

"No...not that I can tell, anyway," Brenda responded. "Still, so much has happened, and it's got me a little shaken."

"I can understand why you'd feel that way."

"Would you have dinner with me tonight? I could really use the company."

"I'm afraid I'm not in town, but I can give you a call later. That's if you'd like to talk."

"Oh. Okay."

He heard the disappointment in Brenda's voice.

Rylee suddenly appeared in the doorway of the office.

Kaleb continued the conversation for a few more minutes before ending the call, his voice trembling with unease. He set his phone down, muttering, "I'm uncertain about how much Brenda is aware of, but her anxiety regarding the agency's recent activities is unmistakable. I can only pray that it's information we can leverage." He glanced up at Rylee. "I wondered where you disappeared to."

"I told you I wouldn't take off again." Rylee looked at him. "Do you think I should start sleeping in the panic room again?"

"Rylee, no one knows you're here."

"You said yourself that the guy with the beard might show up one day… We can't forget that Luis is still out there, looking for me. The cartel already found me at one safe house, and they found you at your place, too. Now John."

He sighed.

"I think it's best if I do this. We don't know whether someone has connected you to me, and you're always telling me that we have to be careful. Well, I'm listening to you."

"Then I'll sleep down here with you." She was right—the threat was closing in all around.

"You don't have to do that. I'll be fine." She gave him a sidelong glance. "Or are you worried that I'll run away again?"

"No, that's not it." Yet that wasn't the truth. Kaleb *was* worried that she would try to take off again. If it hadn't been for Nate tracking her phone, he wasn't sure what would've happened earlier.

"Trust me, I'd rather be upstairs in that nice queen-size bed, but with everything that's happened—it seems like the safest place for me is in a secret room." Rylee rose to her feet. "I'm going to grab my things."

"I'll let Nate know what you've decided."

"Kaleb, are you sure you want to do this? Give up a nice, comfortable bed?"

"We're a team, right?"

She nodded.

And yet she'd almost skipped town without him. Kaleb couldn't believe Rylee had been about to buy a car. He knew how much she wanted to leave Wisconsin, but she needed to be patient.

He was not going to let her out of his sight until she was safe.

KALEB WALKED OUT of the church at the end of John's memorial service on Saturday afternoon. His wife had opted for a private family burial earlier that morning.

He sat down beside Nova before the service started. Kaleb considered her a sister because of his close relationship with her parents.

He swallowed his amusement at the look Nova gave him.

"I see you've picked up a shadow," Nova whispered on the way outside the sanctuary. "What's going on between you and Brenda?"

He whispered his response, almost a sigh. "Nothing. What do you know about her?"

A look of uncertainty crossed her face as she considered the question. "Not much. She's a decent administrative assistant—talks way too much, but she's harmless. One thing's for sure…she's got her eye on you."

He glanced over his shoulder to see if Brenda was still talking to her coworker. Kaleb hoped to make it to his car and be gone by the time she walked out of the church. He didn't want the attention, and it was seeming less and less like she knew anything that could help him find the leak or what happened to John.

A conversation between two other agents caught his attention.

"I heard that John was killed by the same person who murdered Easton… John was hiding the witness…"

"I heard that this was about his money," the other individual offered. "All about greed."

Before Kaleb prepared to leave, John's widow confronted him.

"I'm very sorry for your loss," Kaleb said.

"I remember you, Kaleb," she responded. "I know you and

my husband weren't exactly friends but he was once your partner. Please find out who murdered John."

"Did you notice if he seemed troubled by anything?"

"Something was bothering him, but he wouldn't talk to me about it." Lowering her voice, she said, "I did overhear him talking to someone on the phone the day he died. He mentioned that WITSEC had a leak."

"Anything more?"

"Just that he was planning to meet with you."

"John never showed up," Kaleb responded. "I'll do what I can to find out who is responsible."

Brenda caught up with him after he walked Nova to her car. "That was a beautiful service, don't you think?"

He nodded. "It was."

Dabbing at her left eye with a tissue, she said, "My heart just broke up when John's wife got up to speak. It's obvious she really loved him."

Kaleb didn't know how to respond to her statement.

"Don't mind me. I'm just a romantic at heart," Brenda said.

"So I see."

His eyes bounced around, looking…for what he didn't know. His gaze landed on each face there. Somebody there knew who'd killed John.

Kaleb glanced at Nova, who was watching them in her car. He could read the amusement all over her face. She was clearly enjoying his discomfort.

"I've been trying to sort out all this," Brenda stated. "I was thinking that maybe you could help me."

"Sure," Kaleb responded. "I can try."

"If you can spare some time tomorrow, I'd like to meet for lunch."

"How about noon?"

Brenda smiled. "Perfect. I'll see you tomorrow."

Kaleb started to feel on edge as soon as he left the church parking lot. He glanced in the rearview mirror. There weren't any signs of a car driving too close or staying behind him.

Maybe I'm just being paranoid.

He looked into the rearview mirror a second time. Nothing seemed out of the ordinary, but the feeling wouldn't go away. Kaleb decided to take precautionary measures by not going straight back to Whitefish Bay.

He parked in a shopping center and sent his brother a text.

Delay in coming to the house. Feel like I'm being followed. Don't tell Rylee.

Kaleb surveyed the parking lot. He got out of the car and walked to a café, where he ordered a muffin and coffee.

He sat there for an hour.

When he returned to the car, Kaleb drove the rest of the way to his brother's house, taking a long and meandering route back. He continued to check to see if he was being followed. Still, nothing seemed out of the ordinary.

When Kaleb arrived home, he found Rylee and Nate playing chess.

"Who's winning?"

"Checkmate," Rylee said. "I just won."

Nate shrugged in nonchalance. "I've never been any good at chess."

Rylee glanced at him. "How was the memorial service?"

"It was nice. No one had anything but great things to say about John." Kaleb sat down in a nearby chair.

"Was Brenda there?" she asked.

"Yeah. And she invited me to have lunch with her tomorrow. She wants me to help her sort out what's going on at the agency."

Rylee gave him a sidelong glance. "Surely you're not surprised?"

"No, I'm not. I have to say that I don't think she'll be of any help to us. Whatever lead we might have had died with John."

"You might be right," she responded. "But we're not going to give up."

"No, we're not."

His emotions for Rylee were growing and intensifying. However, Kaleb couldn't afford to let his personal feelings get in the way. It was a challenge to keep her safe and keep her from taking off on her own. He had little time for anything else.

Chapter Fourteen

Rylee had tossed and turned most of the night because of her confusing thoughts and inability to get comfortable. She peered at the clock. It was seven fifteen in the morning.

Kaleb had feelings for Brenda. She had no right being bothered. But she was, and Rylee told herself it was because no one in the marshals' office could be trusted.

Unable to go back to sleep, she decided to get up and start her day.

Rylee glanced over at Kaleb, who was still sleeping. She eased out of bed and tiptoed into the bathroom.

When she walked out, he was awake.

"Where are you going?" he asked.

"To the kitchen. I'm about to make breakfast."

"What time is it?"

"Almost seven forty."

"Why are you up so early?"

"I couldn't sleep," Rylee responded.

She left the panic room and made her way to the kitchen to make spinach, tomato and mushroom omelets. She added fresh fruit.

When the two brothers walked into the kitchen, she handed each of them a plate.

"Kaleb, do you really think it's a good idea to keep spending time with a woman who works in the same office that leaked my location?"

"She likes to talk," he responded. "I'm hoping Brenda will tell me something that might lead to some solid information."

"Do you honestly think an *administrative assistant* is going to know any deep, dark secrets?" She carried her plate over to the breakfast table and sat down across from Nate.

"You never know…" Kaleb glanced down at his plate. "This looks really delicious."

She smiled at him in gratitude.

After breakfast, Rylee sat down with her tablet and reviewed the information she'd gathered since arriving at Nate's.

She started with a disheartened tone, sharing what she'd just read. "I just came across an article—over the weekend, two trucks were seized. The DEA thought they finally had Calderon, but he managed to slip away again." Her frustration was palpable as she continued, "He's the one responsible for the deaths of Easton and John. I'm certain of it… It's so infuriating."

Kaleb offered reassurance, saying, "Calderon won't remain beyond reach forever."

Rylee sighed, her voice heavy with resignation. "At this moment, it feels like he's winning, though."

After they finished eating, she did her laundry.

"I have someone to clean the house," Nate said when he saw her walking toward the front room with the vacuum cleaner.

"I can't just sit around doing nothing."

"Okay, come with me."

She followed Nate into the office.

"I need to run out for a couple of hours. Do you mind answering the phone? Just take messages for me."

Rylee smiled. "I can do that."

"Great. I have the website already pulled up. It gives you an overview of our services."

"Thanks, Nate."

She sat down at the desk.

Kaleb walked by, then backed up. "What are you doing?"

"Working. Nate had to go out, and he asked me to answer the phone."

"I see."

"I was about to clean the house from top to bottom."

He chuckled. "I guess there isn't a lot for you to do."

Rylee sighed. "No, there's not."

The telephone rang.

"I've got to get back to work," she said with a grin.

Smiling, he said, "You do that."

When Nate returned, he asked, "Were there any calls?"

"Six," Rylee responded. "I have all the information right here. I never realized how many people use private security."

"More than most people know, but we don't take on just anybody. Kaleb and I are very selective when it comes to our clientele."

"I suppose you'd have to be," Rylee said.

"We've had a couple of people approach us with question-able backgrounds. We turned them down."

At eleven thirty, Kaleb walked into the family room say-ing, "I'm about to meet Brenda for lunch."

"Have a good time," Rylee replied.

"Thanks. I don't intend to be gone long."

When he left, she told Nate, "I really hope your brother knows what he's doing."

"He does."

Despite his reassurance, Rylee wasn't convinced. Deep down, she believed Kaleb was attracted to Brenda. It would explain why he was so willing to risk their safety. When he came home, she would have a talk with him. If he insisted on seeing Brenda, then Kaleb left her no choice but to take her life into her own hands.

RYLEE HAD JUST walked into the living room when a warning prickled at the back of her neck. She stole a peek outside and saw a man parked in a car across the street watching the house. She couldn't get a good look at his face because of the hood of his coat.

Moving quickly, she ran to the library, where Nate was going through some paperwork, and said, "A man is watching your house. He's parked across the street."

"C'mon…"

She didn't hesitate to follow him.

Nate pressed his shoulder into the frame of the bookcase. The hidden door swung open without a sound.

They slipped inside.

Nate locked the door from the inside. His shallow breathing cut through the silence.

Rylee sat on the edge of the bed while he remained standing. They stared at a twenty-four-inch monitor showing images of several areas in the house. They watched as the man approached the house, the hood shielding his face.

He knocked on the front door and waited.

No answer.

Instead of knocking a second time, he pulled out a small container.

"What's he doing?" Rylee asked as they watched the man on-screen.

"It looks like he's trying to break into the house."

"He doesn't know that he's being videotaped," she uttered.

"He's got his face covered by the hood," Nate said. "He's not worried about being caught."

The uninvited guest opened the door and entered with a gun raised to shoulder level, tiptoeing to keep the boots he wore from reverberating off the hardwood floors.

When he pulled back his hood, Rylee gasped. "That's Luis," she uttered. "How in the world does this man keep finding me?" She glanced at Nate. "Do you think someone put a tracker on Kaleb's car?"

"Possibly. I'll have him check." Nate sent a quick text to his brother. "He could've been followed back to the house the day he left John's memorial service."

"Where are you, Rolanda…Rylee…whatever you're calling yourself these days?" Luis called out. "I want you to know I'm still sore from that car accident. But as you can see, there's nowhere to hide… I will always find you."

He moved deeper into the house.

"C'mon out, pretty lady… I just wanna talk to you," Luis taunted. "We can have some fun, you know…"

Rylee felt sick to her stomach.

"He seems to think you're alone in the house," Nate said. "That means he must know Kaleb's not here."

"That's a good thing, I guess." She sat in the chair, her fingers clenched tightly in her lap. "I just want to know how he figured I was with your brother."

"Whoever is the leak, they must know about Kaleb's friendship with Easton. They knew he'd go to my brother if he felt he couldn't trust anybody else."

They continued to watch Luis as he wandered around the house.

"He'll never find this room," Nate reassured her.

"Can you get phone service in here?" Rylee asked. "And is the room soundproof?"

"Yeah, to both questions," Nate responded. "I just sent a text to Kaleb."

"How long do you think Luis is going to hang around?"

"No idea, but we can wait him out. We have everything we need in here. I made sure of that."

Rylee turned her attention back to the monitor, watching as Luis crept down the hallway, toward the bedrooms at the back of the house. He paused to open a bathroom door. He muttered a string of curses when he found no one there.

He checked every room, then entered the office but walked back out, likely because there were no visible hiding places.

Luis went back through each of the bedrooms, going through the closets and drawers.

"I'm assuming he's looking for your clothes," Nate said. "He wants proof that his information is correct."

"Where are you?" Luis yelled when he couldn't find anything that might belong to her. He returned to the living room and sat down in a chair by the fireplace. Pulling out his phone, he made a call. "You sure this is the right address? The only clothing here belongs to a man. If Kaleb Stone has her, he's not keeping her here. She wasn't at the other house in Milwaukee, either. Yes, I'm sure she's not here."

So, he *was* at the safe house when Easton was attacked. Was he the man who'd shot Easton? She seethed as Luis made himself comfortable in the living room.

"Is he seriously going to wait for Kaleb here?" Rylee asked, pulling her weapon out of her backpack. "I should go out there and take him out right now."

Nate eyed her gun for a moment, then said, "Let my brother take care of Luis."

She stiffened at his words. "I didn't become a marine or an HSI agent to sit on the sidelines, Nate. I know how to handle myself."

"I've no doubt," he responded as he retrieved his own gun from a nearby drawer. "But Kaleb wants you to stand down."

"What are you doing?"

"Preparing to have my brother's back should it come to that."

"And I have yours," Rylee responded. Her tone brooked no argument. "I'm not letting another person die for me."

Chapter Fifteen

"Who are you, and what are you doing in my house?" Kaleb asked calmly when he entered. Nate had already informed him that the intruder was here, and he'd been prepared the moment he stepped inside. "I'm sure you know it's against the law to break into someone's home."

"Kaleb Stone...you have something I want," the man responded.

"I see you know my name. Who are *you*?"

"My name isn't important. Just tell me where she is."

"Who?"

"Where's the woman?"

"Which one?"

Luis's mouth took on an unpleasant twist. "I don't have time for games."

"You found time to break into my house, so why don't you tell me who sent you and what you want?"

"I've been authorized to offer you a million dollars for Rolanda Green. Don't bother lying to me. I know you have her stashed somewhere. All you have to do is give me the address and the money is yours."

"Really?" Kaleb said. "Too bad I don't know anybody by that name."

"Maybe you know her as Rylee Greenwood. This is not the time for you to try and be a hero."

"I don't have any clients by either one of those names. Why don't you tell me why you're looking for this woman?"

Luis chuckled. "Okay, let's say you don't have her, but you do know where she is, don't you? You and that US marshal were real close. I'm sure he mentioned his little witness."

"Easton and I never discussed his job," Kaleb responded. "You never answered my question. Why are you looking for this woman? What is your connection to her?"

"What if I told you that she's my wife?"

He met Luis's gaze straight on. "I'd have to say I don't believe you."

He held up a photo. "This is the person I'm looking for. I'm authorized to offer you a nice sum of money."

"I want you to leave while you still can," Kaleb stated. "I've no interest in accepting your offer. I've already told you that I've never seen that woman."

"She means nothing to you. What does it matter? Think about what you could do with a million dollars."

"Get out of my house," Kaleb demanded.

"Unfortunately, it's not gonna be that easy." Luis got up and pointed his gun at Kaleb. "You really should've taken the money."

"I wouldn't live long enough to spend it."

"True."

Suddenly, a shot rang out.

Luis looked shocked as the tiny red dot on his chest grew larger. He turned around to see the shooter, shock registering on his face. He collapsed on the floor.

Kaleb and Nate eyed one another.

His brother laid his gun on a nearby table. "I've already called the police. They're on the way. The paramedics, too."

Kaleb kicked Luis's gun out of the man's reach, then knelt to check his pulse. "He's still breathing."

Nate checked his pockets. "No identification."

Luis gasped, then slowly opened his eyes.

"They won't s-stop l-looking for her," he said in a hoarse voice.

"I have no idea who you're talking about," Kaleb said. "Whatever this is—leave me out of it."

Luis swallowed hard. He opened his mouth to speak again.

"Save your breath," Kaleb said. "The paramedics and the police should be here soon."

"They're here," Nate announced as he stood in the doorway.

Kaleb kept his eye on the man bleeding on the carpet.

There was soon a flurry of activity as paramedics and police officers entered the house.

"Do you know this guy?" one of the officers asked while EMTs were working on Luis.

"No, I don't," Kaleb responded. "He broke into the house, claiming to be looking for someone. I asked him to leave, and he refused. He pulled a gun on me. My brother arrived home and was able to ease up behind him. He fired on him because this guy was about to shoot me."

"What do you do for a living?" one of the police officers asked.

"We own a private security firm. I used to be a US marshal," Kaleb stated.

"So, you don't know who this guy was looking for? Maybe it was someone you knew when you were with the marshals."

"I haven't been a marshal in a long time. He pulled a gun on me when I told him he'd come to the wrong place. He would've killed me if my brother hadn't come home."

"I checked his pockets," Nate stated, "and he didn't have identification on him. I'm pretty sure he's a hired killer. Maybe someone wants my brother dead."

"Are you sure you didn't make any enemies when you were with the marshals?" the officer questioned.

"I won't say that, but I'm telling you that I never had any dealings with that dude," Kaleb said. "I'd remember. Most of my clients are celebrities or high-profile VIPs."

"Who did he come here looking for?" the officer asked.

"A woman," Kaleb responded. "Rolanda… Yolanda… somebody."

"You live here?" the officer asked.

"No, but I've been staying here for the past couple of weeks. I came to spend some time with my brother. This is Nate's house… I guess this guy came to the wrong place." The officer continued to take full statements from both Nate and Kaleb.

Kaleb glanced over his shoulder at Luis, who was now unconscious. "We need to get him to the hospital," one of the paramedics said.

An officer handcuffed Luis to the gurney before he was wheeled out of the house.

"I can come down to the station if necessary," Nate offered.

"This seems pretty cut-and-dry, and we've got your statements," the officer told him.

His brother walked out with the officer. They stood on the porch talking.

Kaleb yearned to go to Rylee but thought it was better to wait until it was only him and Nate at the house.

"We can't stay here any longer," Nate stated. "The house has been compromised. Did you find a tracking device on your car?"

"No," Kaleb said. "I checked inside and outside…and nothing's on my clothing."

Nate looked perplexed. "At some point someone must have followed you here."

He thought about the sensation he'd had the day of John's

service. He had a feeling Rylee was correct—he'd unknowingly led Luis straight to the house.

Unfortunately, it was no longer safe for her to stay in Whitefish Bay. She was about to get her heart's desire—they were leaving Wisconsin.

SHE SAW THE police leave the house right before Kaleb entered the panic room.

Rylee rushed into his arms, her stomach still clenched tight. Sheer black fright had swept through her when she thought Luis was about to shoot Kaleb. She had pleaded with Nate to let her go out there, but he'd flatly refused.

"I'm glad you're okay," she said. "Luis was going to kill you."

"I know," Kaleb said. "But I knew one or both of you would stop him in his tracks. I wasn't worried."

He was staring as if assessing her.

"Really, I'm fine."

"We need to get moving," he said. "Because once they find out about Luis, they'll send somebody else."

Arms folded across her chest, Rylee responded, "I'm already packed."

"It won't take me more than ten minutes."

Rylee was thrilled about leaving Wisconsin. She was finally heading home.

While Kaleb packed, she went back through the panic room, making sure she'd left nothing behind.

It didn't take long for him to come down with a backpack and suitcase.

Watching him, a panic like she'd never known before welled up in her. The surge of affection she felt toward Kaleb also frightened her.

She was nothing more than a client to Kaleb.

"I HAVE A QUESTION. Why didn't you tell the police about me?" Rylee asked as they put their luggage in the vehicle.

"Because you're supposed to be dead," Kaleb stated. "For now, let's keep it that way. The less people who know that you're alive, the safer you'll be."

She nodded. "When they run Luis's name—he's probably left enough bodies that he'll land in prison for the rest of his life. Do you think he'll try to get a deal?"

Kaleb shook his head no. "Luis doesn't strike me as the type. He'll die before giving up the cartel."

They went back into the house just as Nate came down with a suitcase.

He placed it at the bottom of the stairs, saying, "I'm picking up Rylee's new ID and Social Security number in a couple of hours. Why don't I meet you in Colorado? A friend of mine has a place there that we can use as a safe house. I'll text you the address on your other phone."

"What about the police?" Rylee asked. "What if they have more questions for you?"

Kaleb headed toward the garage. "We'll just tell them that we're out of town on business. Once I have you somewhere safe, I can fly back if necessary."

He and Nate had a short conversation before going their separate ways.

"I hate that you and your brother are going through so much trouble for me," Rylee said as they drove away. "Y'all shouldn't even be mixed up in this."

"If Easton hadn't called me…"

"I'd be on my own," she finished for him. "Don't get me wrong—I appreciate everything you and Nate have done. I don't want anything to happen to either one of you. Every time I think of Easton sacrificing his life for me, it makes me sick inside."

"That's the type of man he was, Rylee. In all his years, Easton never lost a witness. I can't say the same."

"Kaleb, I'm sure what happened wasn't your fault."

"I still blame myself. I should've known what he was doing. He never wanted to stay in witness protection. Said it wasn't for him."

"Then you would've lost him anyway," Rylee pointed out. "He was going to be on his own."

He agreed.

"It sounds like he made choices that cost him his life. There wasn't anything you could do to protect a man who was so reckless."

"I know you're right."

"After we meet Nate in Colorado, what then? Are we heading to Los Angeles?"

"Yeah," Kaleb responded. "That's the plan."

Seemingly satisfied, Rylee settled back in the passenger seat.

"I should've listened to you," he said. "If I'd taken you straight to LA, maybe John would still be alive."

"And maybe not," she responded. "It's very possible that John knew who leaked my information and that's why he was killed. Nobody knows for certain that you and I are together. They didn't find me the night Easton was killed. Luis made a phone call while waiting for you—he told someone that I wasn't in Nate's house. We should be safe."

Kaleb wished he could assure Rylee of their safety, but he could not. They didn't know the identity of the person responsible for the breach, which meant they were still very much in danger.

Chapter Sixteen

The cold morning air emptied Rylee's head of all thoughts as she enjoyed being outside of safe houses and panic rooms.

Once they crossed into Illinois, they stopped at a nearby mall so Rylee could purchase a few clothing items.

"I'd hoped to be home by now," she said, fingering the fringe on a knit scarf.

"I know," Kaleb said.

After a quick lunch of burgers and milkshakes, they got back on the road.

His phone rang.

"It's Brenda," he told Rylee.

She rolled her eyes heavenward but kept her thoughts to herself. Rylee was surprised when he let the call go to voice mail. She knew Kaleb harbored thoughts of gleaning information from her.

"Why are you ghosting her?"

"I'm not. I'll give her a call later."

"Oh, I get it. You want privacy…" She stared out the window. "Why don't you just admit that you're falling in love with Brenda?"

He knew she was teasing and burst into laughter.

Rylee was quiet for the next half hour.

"What are you thinking about?" he inquired.

"I was thinking that I've forgotten what it feels like to date," she said. "It's been a while."

Kaleb glanced over at her. "Missing your social life?"

"It's not like I had much of one before, but yeah… I'd like to see a movie or go to dinner…all the things we take for granted."

"Before WITSEC, I bet you were turning down dates right and left."

"Not really," Rylee responded. "I think some guys found me intimidating."

"I guess I can see that," Kaleb said. "We've got a long drive ahead of us, so what should we talk about?"

She broke into a grin. "How about you tell me about the worst date you've ever been on?"

He looked over at her. "Only if you tell me about yours."

"Deal."

"Okay… I met this girl when I first joined the marines. On our first date, I took her to dinner at this fancy restaurant—I wanted to impress her. She ordered the most expensive meal on the menu, ate most of it, then said she didn't like it. She wanted to order a different entrée until I told her that she'd have to pay for it."

Rylee gave a short laugh. "I'm sure that went over well."

"She was hot with me. We ended up in this debate about women who order meals on dates they wouldn't otherwise pay for themselves. But there was an important lesson in this for me," Kaleb said. "I learned not to take a date to a restaurant that will cost me more than I'm willing to spend."

"My situation is eerily similar," Rylee responded. "My date ordered the most expensive wine, entrée and dessert, then when the check came, he acted like he'd left his wallet at home. I told him I'd pay for my meal, but I wasn't about to pay for his. Suddenly the wallet came out. We each paid for our own meals. Then he had the nerve to ask me out a second time. I told him to lose my number."

"What's the best date you've ever had?"

"When my date booked an entire restaurant just for the two of us. The chef prepared a special six-course meal for us. It was my birthday. Earlier that day, he'd sent me the most beautiful white roses. When he picked me up, he had a corsage of white roses for me." Rylee smiled at the memory. "No one had ever done anything like that for me. He took me to some of the best restaurants all over. Once, he took me to New York just for dinner. Other times, it was Vegas and Miami. He owned his own plane."

"So, you had some rich tycoon wining and dining you."

"He was a stockbroker."

"What happened?"

Rylee glanced over at him. "As it turns out, he was a bit of a jerk once I got to know him better. Very controlling."

"My best date was with a young woman I met while I was in training for the marshals. I was at the FLETEC, the Federal Law Enforcement Training Center in Georgia. She was a local I'd met in the shoe department of a store. She was so sweet, and she knew I was pining for a home-cooked meal. One Sunday, she called and invited me over for dinner. When I arrived, she greeted me with a plant for my room. She made all my favorites. She even made me a lemon pound cake."

"That was really sweet," Rylee said. "What happened with her?"

"She couldn't see herself living anywhere but in that town. She was very close to her family. I knew it wasn't a place I wanted to live, so we decided to be friends. She got married a year later."

"So, she was the one who got away?"

"No. I cared for her, but it wasn't a forever kind of love."

"Oh," Rylee murmured. "Have you ever felt that way about anybody?"

Instead of responding to her question, Kaleb posed one of his own. "What is your ideal type of man?"

"My perfect man is someone who has a beautiful soul and is kindhearted but also has an inner strength. He's not the type to put people down or bully others and can see the beauty of everyone around him. He knows that people have flaws, including himself. What about you, Kaleb? What do you look for in a woman?"

"She's honest and never apologizes for it. I want a woman who will call things as she sees them, and she'll always speak the truth in a loving way. I value those qualities above all else."

Kaleb glanced over at her, his gaze raking boldly over her.

The smoldering flame she saw in his eyes surprised Rylee but sent her spirits soaring.

THEY ARRIVED AT their destination in Denver after fifteen long hours on the road.

Weary, Kaleb turned off the high-tech alarm system. "There are two guest rooms upstairs. We'll sleep up there."

"What? No panic room?" Rylee asked.

Kaleb laughed. "Actually, there is one—it's in the billiards room."

"Did Nate design this house, too?"

He nodded. "He did."

Rylee continued to look around. "When do you think your brother will get here?"

Checking his watch, Kaleb said, "Within the next hour."

"You know you should call Brenda back," Rylee stated.

"I probably should." But all Kaleb wanted to do was grab a nap.

She headed toward the kitchen. "I'm going to see what's in the pantry while you make your call."

When Rylee returned, Kaleb was off the phone.

They made small talk while preparing a meal together.

Thirty minutes later, they sat down to eat.

"I'll clean up," Rylee said. "I know you're tired from all the driving."

"I'm fine," he responded. "This meal has energized me."

She chuckled. "It's a hamburger."

"It did the job," Kaleb said with a grin. "I never had one with avocado. I liked it."

"I'm surprised you could taste it—you had it buried under the onions, tomato and bacon," Rylee responded. "Not to mention the lettuce."

"I wasn't sure how I'd like it, so I tried one slice."

They both decided to go to bed early. Kaleb escorted Rylee to her room.

"I hope you can get back your old life," he said while standing in the hallway.

"I'm going to get it back," she responded with determination.

There was a tingling in the pit of her stomach as he moved closer to her. Rylee's heart jolted as he took another step.

When he gathered her into his arms, Kaleb's mouth covered hers hungrily, but he was surprisingly gentle, too.

Rylee looked up at Kaleb, and he gazed at her in a way that left her breathless. He placed a hand on her chin, then leaned forward to claim her lips again.

He kissed her and she responded, their kiss building in intensity. Kaleb kissed her a third time, and she allowed all her pent-up feelings to be revealed.

Rylee began to pull back, but he wrapped his arms around her, pulling her close to him.

"Kaleb…"

"Don't say it," he whispered.

Without looking away, Rylee backed out of his grasp. "We need to stay focused and alert."

He nodded in agreement. "You're right."

She stepped away, giving herself a mental shake.

Stay focused.

THE KISS SHE'D shared with Kaleb was still on her mind the next day. She took a few minutes to consider what her life could look like with him in it. She told herself that she'd have to settle for this one moment they'd shared.

We can't let our guard down now, she reminded herself. It was imperative that they stay focused—doing so would keep everyone safe.

She shook her head. "I can't let that happen again."

Kaleb was downstairs in the kitchen when she came down the stairs.

Rylee grabbed a bag of potato chips and opened it.

"Chips for breakfast?" he asked.

She nodded. "Yep. Comfort food."

"You play chess, right?"

"I do."

"Interested in playing a game with me later? I noticed a chessboard in the billiards room. Just so you know, I'm much better than my brother," Kaleb said.

"I learned how to play during my time in Racine. The restaurant where I worked held chess tournaments. I knew Easton played, so I decided to see what was so great about this game. Turns out, I really enjoy it."

"Easton taught me the game," Kaleb said. "I tried to teach Nate, but I'm not that good a teacher."

A few minutes into the game, he stated, "You're pretty good at this."

She smiled. "Thank you. I even beat Easton."

Kaleb looked surprised. "What…really? I'm sure his ego took a hit."

"He couldn't believe it," Rylee said with a chuckle. Kaleb grinned, and she had to tear her eyes away from his lips.

There was no denying that she wanted him to kiss her again.

I can't do this. I can't fall in love with this man. Our relationship is purely professional.

"You okay?" he asked.

"Huh?" She was stalling because she wasn't sure of what would come out of her mouth.

"I asked if you're okay."

"I'm fine," Rylee said. She got up and walked over to the fireplace to look at the photographs on the mantel. She needed to put some distance between them.

Kaleb joined her.

Rylee picked up one of a couple with their three children. "Nice-looking family," she murmured. "They look happy and peaceful."

"They do."

"Kaleb, that's what I want—a happy and peaceful life."

"Then you may have to give up going back to Homeland Security."

"I had it before, and I can have it again. I just have to be intentional about it."

He looked down at her. "The more I get to know you… I wouldn't be surprised."

Rylee reminded herself to stay focused. She took a few slow breaths and tried to persuade her rapidly beating heart to return to normal. She had to look away from those beautiful eyes and his sensual lips. She couldn't kiss him again. It wouldn't be fair to either of them.

Chapter Seventeen

Kaleb felt a thread of relief when his brother finally arrived. He wasn't the only one. Rylee practically squealed with delight upon seeing Nate. He swallowed his envy over the way she threw herself into his brother's arms.

"Did you run into any problems before leaving Wisconsin?" Kaleb asked.

"None. I did speak with the police," he responded. "When and if Luis recovers, he's going to prison. I also heard that DEA and FBI are both wanting to take him into custody."

"That's great to hear," Rylee stated. "It's a small win, but a win nonetheless. When I get to LA, I plan to meet with my supervisor as soon as we get there. I intend to get my job back."

"Does he know that you're alive?"

"I don't think so," she responded. "It was the special agent in charge's decision. Once I speak with Burns, I'm sure he'll be told."

After Nate was settled, they ordered food. Thankfully, Denver's rush hour wasn't in full effect.

Kaleb paid close attention to Rylee's conversation with Nate, wondering if she was attracted to him. It would pain him, but if her affections were for his brother, he'd have no choice but to stay out of the way.

It didn't take long for the food to arrive. Both Nate and

Rylee had ordered the crab cakes, while Kaleb ordered a burger.

"When do you plan to leave?" Nate asked as he picked up his fork.

"First thing in the morning," Kaleb responded.

Rylee sliced into her crab cake. "I can't wait to get home. Nate, I wish you were coming with us."

"Not this trip," he responded.

She glanced over at Kaleb and smiled. "You okay?"

Kaleb downed some of his water.

"I ran another thorough search on the car, and still, no sign of any GPS trackers. I've checked my clothes, combed through everything."

Rylee nodded, her frustration evident. "I did the same thing. Went through my backpack and suitcase with a fine-tooth comb. I just can't fathom how they keep locating us."

Nate chimed in, sharing their bewilderment. "None of my equipment picked up anything either."

Rylee met his gaze. "Maybe it fell off or something."

"I'M EXHAUSTED, so I think I'll go to bed," Rylee announced, looking away. She still couldn't forget how Kaleb's mouth had felt over hers, and the more time she spent with him, the more she dreamed of kissing him again.

She stretched and yawned.

"I'll see you in the morning," Kaleb said. "We'll be hitting the road around nine."

His gaze was warm as it lingered on her.

"Good night, you two," she said.

Rylee rose to her feet and headed toward the stairs.

"Sweet dreams," he replied.

As she prepared for bed, Rylee could hear Kaleb and his brother talking and laughing downstairs.

She loved the sound of his laughter and the fact that they shared the same sense of humor. Kaleb got her and she got him. But it could never be anything more than what it was. Rylee had to force herself to stop thinking about him and the future they would never have.

THE NEXT MORNING, Rylee came downstairs to find Nate and Kaleb sitting in the living room talking. She placed her backpack and suitcase near the door.

"Nate, when are you planning to leave?"

"Tomorrow morning," he responded. "I'm planning to spend some time on vacation in Canada. I'll head back to Whitefish Bay in a couple weeks."

"What if they send someone else to the house?"

"I own another place there—that's where I'll be staying for the time being. The police are planning to patrol the area. But if they do return, they'll find the house empty."

"I don't want anything to happen to either one of you."

"We're good," Kaleb responded. "We're all going to come out of this alive."

She smiled at him. "Agreed."

One glance out the living room window made her bones chill. It was a blustery day, the wind blowing with the briskness of winter. What she needed right now was a nice hot cup of tea. Maybe that would banish the chill that threatened to overtake her.

She boiled water in a teakettle, hoping a warm drink on the road might settle the unease she suddenly felt.

While she waited for the water to boil, her thoughts drifted to Kaleb. He stirred something in her, something that had never been stirred before. He made Rylee think of all the things she hadn't thought of before…like love, marriage and children. There hadn't been time for those kinds of thoughts before, those kinds of yearnings, because she was building her career as an HSI special agent. She'd always assumed she'd have all that eventually once her career was solid. It was only since she'd met Kaleb that this strange, foreign wistfulness welled up in her, a vague desire for something more in her life, something more than what Rylee had now, something more than being in law enforcement.

The tea didn't help. It didn't warm Rylee, nor did it take away any of the edgy tension that had been her shadow for the last couple of days.

"Time for us to get going," Kaleb said when she left the kitchen with her tea. She offered the brothers a cup, but they declined.

Rylee hugged Nate. "I hope to see you again."

He smiled. "I have a feeling we'll be seeing one another sooner than you can imagine."

"I hope so," she murmured.

Kaleb picked up her suitcase. "We should get going."

Just as they were about to pull out of the driveway, a car blocked their exit.

"This isn't good," Rylee uttered.

The car that had blocked them in was a beat-up old sedan, driven by a scruffy-looking man with dark eyes and a thin mustache.

Concern clouded Kaleb's face as Rylee pulled out her gun. The car blocking their exit was ominous, and she had a gut feeling that things were about to go terribly wrong.

"Stay down," he told her.

"You drive… I got this."

Gunfire burst from the sedan.

She took a deep breath as Kaleb put the car into Reverse.

Rylee fired back, her gun popping in the silence. Kaleb hit the gas, and she felt the car lurch backward as he swerved around the sedan, aiming for the open gate. The car jolted, and she heard the sound of metal crunching as they smashed into the gate, but Kaleb didn't slow down. They needed to get out of there, fast.

The scruffy-looking man stumbled back as the car burst through the gate, his gun smoking as he fired another shot.

Kaleb swerved again, barely avoiding the bullet, then he slammed on the gas, speeding down the street. For a few moments, there was only the sound of their heavy breathing and the squealing of tires as they sped away. Rylee glanced over her shoulder. "I think I hit him with that last round."

"I don't know how they're able to track us so quickly."

"There must be something on this car. We need to get rid of it."

"As soon as it's safe to stop, I'm going to check it again," he responded. "Either way, I agree that we need to switch cars."

Rylee looked behind them. "I don't think he's following us. He most likely needs medical attention."

"But it won't take long for someone else to find us," Kaleb stated.

They parked in front of a convenience store, and she helped him search the vehicle.

Kaleb muttered a curse. "Found it," he said, holding up a tiny device. "It was hidden in the sunroof." He smashed it with his foot.

They took a taxi to a used car lot and purchased a vehicle with cash.

"Are you sure this will get us to California?" Rylee asked, walking around the ten-year-old SUV.

"It should get us to Nevada. I'll pick up a rental there." Kaleb eyed her. "Don't worry. I will get you safely to Los Angeles, as promised."

Chapter Eighteen

"Rylee, you don't have to be so strong all the time," Kaleb said when they were driving on I-15 South toward Las Vegas. "You've been through a lot in a short amount of time. It's okay to show you're shaken—that's normal."

"I'm okay," she responded. "I'm not a victim, Kaleb. It's my mom that I'm worried about. I've been thinking a lot about her. I have no idea what she's been told by the marshals' service. I want her to know I'm okay so that she isn't worrying about me."

"Would you like to call her?" he asked. "The phone is untraceable."

She was stunned and surprised by his offer. "Someone may be listening in—I don't want to jeopardize her."

"They already know that you're alive. Just let her know that you're safe. Nothing else."

Rylee took the phone and keyed in her mother's number. When she heard it ring, she prayed for her mother to answer.

"Mama…"

"Rolanda, are you okay? Baby, it's so good to hear your voice."

"I'm safe. I called so you wouldn't worry. I can't talk long, but know that I love you very much."

She glanced over at Kaleb and smiled.

He didn't regret giving her this moment with her mother. He'd wanted to do something special for her.

"Mama, please don't cry. Everything is going to be fine. Just trust me." She nodded. "Okay… I have to go now, but just know that I'm safe."

She ended the call, then said, "I can't thank you enough. I really needed to hear her voice."

"I know."

Rylee swiped at the lone tear that ran down her cheek.

Kaleb took her hand in his, giving it a gentle squeeze. "We're working on it. You know Nate can arrange for your mother to be taken to a safe house somewhere."

"I think that's a great idea," she responded. "At least I won't have to worry about her."

RYLEE CONVINCED KALEB to let her drive for a while. "You look tired. I know you and Nate were up late last night talking."

"We're about three hundred miles away from Nevada," he said.

"Driving will take my mind off things."

"Okay."

Kaleb took the next exit to a rest area, and they switched seats. He glanced over at her and smiled. "Now, don't go getting any speeding tickets."

"I know you aren't talking about my driving," Rylee said.

Twenty minutes later, Kaleb was sound asleep.

Rylee chuckled to herself. Her feelings for him continued to deepen, but she forced herself to stay focused on getting to Los Angeles.

He woke up forty-five minutes later.

"You want me to take over?" he asked.

"I'm okay right now." She glanced over at him and said, "One thing I've missed most is traveling. I love to see new places. Reading and traveling. Those are my two favorite things to do."

"Same here. I love to travel."

She'd noticed that Kaleb also enjoyed reading. He'd purchased a couple of books on the drive to Denver.

"What's the first thing you're going to do when we get there?"

"Find an In-N-Out. They have the best burgers."

"I'll have to test that theory," Kaleb said. "We have some great burger places in Milwaukee. AJ Bombers is my favorite."

"They're good," Rylee admitted. "But they're no In-N-Out."

"Nevada, yes..." Rylee uttered. "Almost home."

They were still seven and a half hours away from Los Angeles, so he suggested, "Why don't we get a room for the night? We can both get some rest and start out early in the morning."

They found a hotel near Beaver Dam State Park. "We're in the middle of nowhere," Rylee said. "I want my own room."

"Okay, but we're getting adjoining rooms, and you have to leave the connecting door unlocked."

"I can do that," she said.

After checking in, they ordered food from a nearby restaurant and sat to eat.

"I wish I could play the slot machines when we get to Vegas," Rylee stated. "I've missed my weekend trips with my friends there. We used to have so much fun. Sometimes, my mom would join us."

"Have your parents always lived on the West Coast?"

She nodded. "Both born and raised in Cali. My mom grew up in Los Angeles, but my dad was from Oakland. His family moved to LA when he was sixteen. That's when my parents met. They lived a block away from one another."

"High school sweethearts."

Rylee nodded a second time. "My dad was a police officer. He was killed in the line of duty when I was fifteen. My brother never got over losing our father. I think it's why he turned to drugs. It was the only way he could cope." She released a sad sigh. She knew that he'd understand when she said, "I want to take as many drug dealers off the streets as possible. However, the reality is that when you take down one, two more seem to pop up. It's a never-ending battle."

"It's like the mythical creature...the Hydra. You cut off one head and another grows in its place," Kaleb responded.

Rylee agreed.

"One of the things I really like about you is that you trust your gut regardless."

"It's never led me wrong. The day my father died, I could feel something was about to happen. I didn't want him to go to work. I pleaded with him to just stay home..." She shook off the memory. "After Raul died, I thought I was safe, so I began letting my guard down.

"The night Luis came into the restaurant—I just knew he was there looking for me. In fact, all that week, I felt a strange sensation. At times, I felt like I was being watched, but I chalked it up to being paranoid."

"Tell me about this task force idea of yours."

"I've spent a lot of my time studying the reports of previous joint operations and made note of what worked and didn't work... We need an interagency operation all working together to take down the cartel. ATF, DEA, FBI and Homeland Security. Working together to fight a common enemy. It's worked in the past. One of the first things we need is a group of IT experts. We can even call it Operation Reckoning. I already know a couple of people who would be great assets to the team. One is a DEA agent and the other HSI."

"How long have you been working on this?"

"Since I've been in WITSEC. It's the only thing that's kept me going. I never intended to go quietly into the night. I intend to keep striking at the Mancuso cartel until I get Calderon locked up."

Kaleb met her gaze. "I admire your determination. Though so far, we haven't figured out much."

"I'm not ready to give up."

"Then neither am I."

Rylee smiled. "Like I said…we make a great team. So, we know for sure that there is a leak in the marshals' service. Now that John Martin is dead, what are your thoughts, Watson?"

Kaleb chuckled. "Did you just make me your sidekick?"

"Well, if I'm Sherlock…I guess that would be a yes."

He stroked his chin in a thoughtful manner. "I didn't care for John, but he was good at his job. As for why he called that meeting, all we have is speculation, Holmes."

She laughed. "Let's go with the theory that John figured out the identity of the mole."

"Yeah, and it got him killed." He wiped his mouth on a napkin. "What do we do now?"

"We go to Los Angeles," Rylee said. "Calderon already knows I'm alive—we'll come up with an action plan of our own."

"With Sherlock on the case, they'll be on the run in no time," Kaleb teased.

Rylee gave a short laugh. "I guess you think I'm living in a dream world, but I'm not. Kaleb, I know it won't be an easy feat. I'm just not ready to give up." For the next half hour, they chatted with an easy camaraderie.

Kaleb was really a lot of fun. Rylee hadn't laughed this much in a long time. It felt good.

Really good.

WHEN THEY FINISHED EATING, Rylee sat down on the edge of Kaleb's bed, where they continued their conversation.

"Do you have any idea where Calderon could be hiding?" Rylee asked.

"I know he had a compound in Mexico, but when the authorities showed up, there was a shoot-out. Calderon somehow managed to escape."

"I keep thinking if there hadn't been police in that area that night…" She couldn't finish the thought.

"I have to admit that surprises me, too," Kaleb said.

Rylee tried to concentrate on the case, but she couldn't keep her mind off the man seated near her.

"Why have you gone quiet on me?"

"I was thinking about something," she responded.

"You care to share?"

"If Calderon has managed to avoid arrests all this time, I don't know why I believe I can make a difference." Deep down she wasn't sure she could really do it.

"You just may be the one to take him down, Rylee."

She looked over at him. "That's sweet of you to say."

"I mean it."

He pulled her closer to him. Kaleb's mouth covered hers, kissing her thoroughly.

Rylee broke the kiss. "We should stay focused."

"You're right, but I have to confess it's sometimes a challenge. I'm very attracted to you."

"Let's put Calderon and as many of his people behind bars…"

Kaleb nodded in agreement.

"If things were different—" Rylee began.

"I know," he responded.

Chapter Nineteen

The following day, Rylee was up by 6:00 a.m. She was dressed and ready to go by the time Kaleb woke.

"How long have you been up?"

"Since six." She walked over to the mirror and fluffed her curls. Dressed in black jeans and a lightweight black sweater, she said, "It feels good not to have to wear thermal underwear any longer."

Kaleb checked the temperature. "The weather is pretty nice out here."

She gave him an incredulous look. "*Nice*…it's great."

He chuckled. "You look so much happier right now."

"That's because I'm almost home," she murmured.

"I suppose you'd prefer to grab breakfast on the go rather than eat here."

She looked at him, smiling. "If you don't mind."

Kaleb chuckled. "Okay, let's get out of here."

"Have you talked to Nate?" Rylee inquired while they were waiting to check out of the hotel.

"I called him last night. He's having a great time in Canada. He took our parents with him. They're celebrating their fortieth wedding anniversary."

"That's great," she said. "I hope they have a wonderful time. I feel bad for taking you away from your family."

"It's fine," Kaleb said. "Nate gave my parents the gifts I

bought, and I had a chance to speak to them. They understand that our jobs often take us out of town."

She nodded. "The last Christmas before I went into WITSEC, Mom and I went on a cruise with my aunt to Puerto Rico." Rylee grinned. "We had a blast."

"That's something I've always wanted to do. Spend the holiday on a cruise ship."

"You should do it."

As they continued to drive toward the state line, Rylee drifted off to sleep.

She woke up just before they crossed into California.

"We're stopping at the first In-N-Out we see."

Kaleb glanced over at her and laughed. "You were serious about that."

Adjusting her seat, Rylee said, "I'm telling you, it's one of the best hamburgers you'll ever taste."

"Then I'm looking forward to trying one."

"I have a good feeling about this. You're going to love In-N-Out," she stated. "I have to warn you...their burgers can become an addiction." Rylee glanced out the window. "There's one coming up at the next exit."

KALEB COULDN'T DENY IT. The hamburger he'd just eaten was one of the best he'd ever tasted.

"Sooo..." Rylee prompted.

"You were right. It's right up there with AJ's."

She laughed, then finished off the rest of her burger.

Rylee had no idea of the growing fire she'd ignited in him. Kaleb sat there listening while he drank in the comfort of her nearness.

They got back on the road as soon as they finished eating.

When his phone rang, Kaleb asked Rylee to retrieve it from the compartment between them.

"It's Brenda," she announced.

"Hello?"

Kaleb glanced over at Rylee, who made a face. He swallowed his laughter.

"I need to talk to you," came Brenda's voice. "I don't want to do it over the phone. Can we meet?"

"I'm still on the road," Kaleb said. "I'm traveling with a client."

"Are you possibly going to be near the Los Angeles area?"

Kaleb paused a minute, then asked, "Why?"

"I'm taking a few days off to visit family. I'm flying out tonight."

"So you'll be in California?"

Rylee glanced in his direction.

"Just for a few days. If you're gonna be near LA… I thought maybe you could meet me there. We could spend a day or two together."

"I'm in the Midwest," he lied.

There was a pause. "I see."

"It's just been bad timing," he responded. "We can talk by phone while you're on the West Coast." When he ended the call, Rylee asked, "Did I just hear you say that Brenda's coming to Los Angeles?"

"Yeah."

Her eyes narrowed. "Did she ever tell you that she was from LA?"

"I never really asked her, and she never mentioned it— she talked about everything else."

"Hmm…" Rylee uttered. "I don't know, but my gut tells me this isn't coincidental."

"I'm inclined to agree with you," Kaleb stated. "I'm beginning to think that maybe we've found the leak."

"Do you really think it might be Brenda?" Rylee questioned.

"I always felt there was something about her that didn't quite ring true to me," Kaleb responded. "I never trusted the woman. I kept waiting to see if she would eventually show her hand. Knowing what I do about John, if he thought she was the mole, he most likely confronted her. That's what got him killed."

"If she's coming to Los Angeles, there's a reason for it," Rylee stated. "We need to find out what that reason is."

Looking at him, she said, "Kaleb, you're not going to like this, but you need to call Brenda back and tell her that you'll meet her tomorrow. I'll talk to my old supervisor at HSI. If Brenda is connected to the cartel, she may be our way to get some inside information."

Kaleb nodded. "You might be right."

He called Brenda back.

She answered on the second ring, saying, "Hey, I'm on my way to the airport right now."

"I thought about what you said. I talked to my client to let him know that I'm taking a couple of days off, so I'll be able to meet you in Los Angeles after all."

"That's wonderful news, Kaleb. I have reservations at the Marriott in Universal City."

The hair on the back of his neck stood up. "I thought you said you were visiting family out there."

"I am, but it doesn't mean I want to stay with them. I value my peace, if you know what I mean."

"I should get in tomorrow around three."

"Kaleb, thank you for this. I really need to talk to you."

"Let's meet tomorrow night. Dinner around six?"

"Of course," she responded.

Kaleb ended the call. "We need to find out everything we can about Brenda Perez. I tried, but nothing came up that warranted a red flag."

Rylee nodded. "And while you meet her, hopefully my supervisor can have someone plant a wire in her room."

"Turns out Brenda and I had the same agenda—we both wanted information."

KALEB AND RYLEE checked in to the Hilton near the Los Angeles airport. Once they were settled in their rooms, she said, "I spoke to Eric Burns. He's the special agent in charge. After he got over the shock of hearing my voice, he said he wants to meet with us, and he's bringing my former supervisor with him."

"That's great. Where do they want to meet?"

"He's coming to the hotel this evening." Rylee unlocked the door to the adjoining room.

Their visitors arrived a few minutes past seven.

Kaleb opened the door and stepped aside to let them enter.

The special agent in charge walked over to Rylee, greeting her warmly. She looked over at her former supervisor. "It's good to see you, SSA Graham."

Clearing his voice, he responded, "Excuse me for staring, but I still haven't processed the fact that you're alive and well."

"I thought it best that you and the rest of the department thought Rolanda died—her death needed to look real," Burns said.

Graham stated, "Well, I can't tell you how much this thrills me to see you."

"Just call me Rylee," she responded. "I've gotten used to it." She paused a moment before blurting, "You have to know that Stuart wasn't trafficking drugs. I read all about the accusations during the investigation."

"I never once believed that Stuart was dirty—I just couldn't prove it." Graham walked over to the window and peeked out.

"Someone came after me," Rylee stated. "It's why I had to leave WITSEC. The marshals have a leak in their office."

"Deputy US Marshal John Martin in the Milwaukee office reached out to me, but someone killed him before we could meet," Kaleb interjected. "I believe he figured out that Brenda Perez is the leak. I'm having dinner with her tomorrow. I'll pick her up at six. How long will it take you to put a wire in her room?"

"Not long at all," Graham responded. "I can have agents at the hotel before she leaves. I'll even try to have them installed in a room next to hers or close by."

"Perfect," Kaleb responded.

"How's my mother doing?" Rylee asked.

"Daphne misses you terribly," Graham said. "I've been checking on her at least once a month. Does she know you're alive?"

"Yes. They allowed her to see me before I went into the program."

His eyebrows rose in surprise. "Look at that… Daphne never once let on."

"I can't wait to see her."

"Hopefully, this woman will give us some solid intel on the Mancuso cartel," Graham said. "I'll have special agents Jim and Rob come here with you to keep you updated on what's going on."

She smiled in gratitude. "Thank you."

When the two left, Kaleb said, "Burns and Graham both seem like good men."

"They are. I enjoyed working with them. Graham taught me a lot."

"There's no doubt in your mind that they can be trusted?"

"I trust them with my life." Rylee's stomach growled. "I guess I need to eat something."

Kaleb picked up the phone. "I'll order some food for us."

Tears welled up in her eyes as she grasped his hand, her voice quivering with emotion. "Thank you," she whispered, her words heavy with gratitude, "for keeping your word and bringing me to Los Angeles."

Her eyes locked onto his, and her heart pounded in her chest. "Kaleb," she confessed, her voice trembling, "I like you. I like you more than I ever wanted to, and it scares me how much."

"Why?"

"Because we can't afford to be distracted," Rylee stated.

Ten minutes later, there was a knock on the door.

"Our food's here," Kaleb announced.

Removing the cover from her meal, Rylee said, "This looks and smells delicious." She glanced at the baked chicken stuffed with wild rice.

Old-school R & B played softly in the background.

Rylee began swaying as she ate. "I love The Temptations."

"So do I," Kaleb said with a chuckle.

After they finished eating, he coaxed her into a dance.

When Kaleb pulled her into his arms, Rylee felt the sparks in her belly ignite into a flame, the heat spreading through her body.

"I keep thinking about what you said. We do make a great team," he said.

"I agree, Watson."

They moved their bodies to the music, and Kaleb began singing to her.

Looking up into his handsome face, Rylee couldn't speak for a few seconds. She felt like she was dreaming as his words began permeating her mind and soul. When she could speak again, she said, "You have a nice voice, Mr. Stone."

Kaleb planted a kiss on her forehead. She pulled his face

to hers, kissing him passionately, before stepping away. "I'll see you in the morning."

Rylee walked briskly to her room, then closed the door behind her. She had to leave before her resolve melted.

Chapter Twenty

"Are you ready for tonight?" Rylee asked the next morning during breakfast.

"Not really," Kaleb admitted. "I'd rather stay here with you. I'd have more fun."

"Well, there's no denying that," she said with a laugh. "But it won't be too bad…"

"How do you feel about all this?" he asked.

"I don't want anything to happen to you," Rylee responded. "There's a part of me that worries that you may be walking into a trap." He nodded. "You're going to take your gun with you?"

"Of course."

"If I could be there, I'd have your back, Kaleb."

Smiling, he responded, "I know. But you'll be able to hear our conversation. I'm wired for sound."

Rylee snuggled up beside him. "Let's just enjoy the time we have together before you have to leave."

RYLEE HELPED KALEB with his collar.

"Please be careful…" she murmured. "Brenda could be dangerous. She may have been the one who shot John."

Kaleb was touched by her concern. Rylee didn't need to worry, though. He was going to do whatever he had to do to stay safe. Brenda entered his mind, but he quickly chased the image of her away. He didn't want her intruding on his time with Rylee.

"We'll be surrounded by lots of other people."

Narrowing her eyes, Rylee replied, "Uh-huh…you know she's going to try to get you alone. I'm going to lock that door in case she comes back with you."

"That's not going to happen," he assured her. Kaleb had every intention of returning here to spend the rest of the evening with Rylee. They'd had a wonderful morning, and he wanted to end the evening with her.

Rylee kissed him before sending him out the door. "C'mon, Watson…you got this."

"I'll be back as soon as I can."

She nodded. "I'll be here."

He took the elevator downstairs, then walked out to his car.

Kaleb drove to the Universal City hotel and waited in the lobby for Brenda to come down.

He called Rylee to check on her. "Are you okay?"

"Yes. I'm good," she responded. "My Glock is locked and loaded. Jim and Rob should be here within the hour."

"Well, I just arrived," Kaleb said, his voice full of regret.

They hung up. Kaleb walked around the lobby and called Brenda. "Hey, I'm downstairs."

Brenda walked out of the elevator five minutes later. She kissed him on the cheek in greeting. "It's so good to see you. I've been looking forward to this evening all day."

"How does your family feel about your running out on them?"

"They understood. I told them I had a date. Besides, I spent last night and most of the day with them."

He escorted her to the car he'd rented and opened the door for her.

"Thank you," Brenda murmured.

"So is California your home?" Kaleb asked when they were on their way to the restaurant.

"No, not at all," Brenda responded. "I grew up in Philadelphia. After I graduated from college, I came out here to work for a record company. That's how I met my ex-boyfriend. He was a musician."

"How did you end up with the marshals' service in Wisconsin?"

He noticed that her smile vanished for a moment, but Brenda quickly recovered. "My ex grew up in Wisconsin. When his music career didn't pan out, he decided to return home and asked me to come with him. Once I was there, I landed the job with the marshals. I'm glad, because things didn't work out with him. He ended up moving to Chicago with some wannabe singer."

The wave of conversations among the diners in the restaurant ebbed and flowed around them, mingling with the clinking of silverware against plates.

Brenda settled back in her seat. "What made you change your mind about coming to Los Angeles?"

"You did," Kaleb responded. "I wanted to hear what you have to say. Something is obviously bothering you."

She nodded. "I think there's a mole in the marshals' agency. I initially thought it was coming out of our office, but now I'm not so sure. They could be anywhere. There's a witness that had to be moved earlier this week because their identity was compromised."

"Why do you believe this?"

"Because of Easton's death...then John's murder. Easton's witness still hasn't been located—he or she is probably dead. I don't know who to trust in my own office. The only person I can talk to is you."

"The witness who had to be relocated—are they connected to the Mancuso cartel?"

"I believe so," Brenda responded. "But I'm not sure." She leaned forward in her chair. "Kaleb, I'm feeling a little nervous about working at the agency. I'm not sure I feel safe."

"You haven't had any more incidents of someone following you?"

"Not that I can tell and I'm very vigilant. All of this has me a bit shaky. I'm seriously looking for a new job." The server came to the table and told them about the multicourse, Spanish-inspired meal being served.

When he walked away with their orders, Brenda said, "Did you know about the menu?"

Kaleb nodded. "I thought it was something you might enjoy."

She broke into a grin. "You're such a sweetheart."

The first course featured shareable appetizers of Iberico ham and wild mushroom soup.

"This is delicious," Brenda said.

For their entrée, Kaleb chose the butter-roasted monkfish with Manila clams and salsa verde, while Brenda decided on the paella. For dessert they shared a huge slice of cheesecake.

"Kaleb, I want you to know that this has been a wonderful evening. The food…the company…"

He smiled. "I agree. I enjoyed myself."

When Brenda excused herself to visit the ladies' room, Kaleb sent a text to Rylee.

Leaving the restaurant soon. All good?

She responded quickly.

All good to go.

He put his phone away when he saw Brenda coming his direction. He couldn't wait to get back to Rylee.

Smiling, she returned to her seat.

Kaleb stood up. "You ready?"

She stood up and picked up her purse. "Thank you again for coming to LA. I really appreciate it."

When he took her back to her hotel, Brenda got out, saying, "You don't have to walk me in—go get your rest."

"If you think of anything else, don't hesitate to give me a call," Kaleb told her. He couldn't explain it, but there was something about Brenda that did not add up. He hoped to learn more after bugging her hotel room.

"I just wish I could make sense of it all."

He nodded in agreement.

RYLEE OPENED THE door to let Kaleb into her room.

"The gang's all here, I see," he said.

She introduced Kaleb to Jim and Rob before they settled down and waited.

"Okay, she's making a call," Rylee stated.

They sat there, listening.

"*¡Hola!* I saw that you called me earlier, but I couldn't talk. I was having dinner with Kaleb Stone. He's the former marshal I told you about." Brenda giggled. "It's a good thing he's no longer a marshal. I'd never get any work done."

Rylee glanced over at him and chuckled.

He shrugged nonchalantly.

They had no idea who was on the other end of the phone, but Brenda's voice suddenly took on a defensive tone.

"I know what I'm doing," she snapped. "There's nothing to worry about. He doesn't suspect a thing. Remember, *I'm* the one who got Kaleb to come here." Brenda paused momentarily, then said, "And I'm pretty sure he didn't come here alone."

Rylee and Kaleb exchanged glances.

His instincts had never been wrong. He'd had a feeling that she knew much more than she was saying.

"She's the mole," Rylee stated.

Kaleb agreed.

They listened as Brenda said, "No, I don't have proof, but yes…I believe she's here. We have to find a way to draw Rolanda out." Brenda released a sigh. "No, he's not staying here at this hotel. I can't just ask him a bunch of questions like that—I don't want to make him suspicious."

"She's not talking to Calderon," Rylee said. "It could be Poppy."

"Whatever…fine." Brenda huffed. "We're having dinner tomorrow," they heard her say. "I don't think we should risk putting another tracking device on his vehicle—they found the last one. He says he'll be here for a couple days, so basically that's all the time we have to find where Kaleb has her hidden."

The conversation ended.

Rylee looked over at Kaleb. "Well, we know they're still looking for me."

"Could be… I'm more interested in knowing how she plans to draw you out," he said.

"I don't know…" She paused a moment, then said, "The only way they could possibly get to me is through my mom… Kaleb, we need to take her someplace safe."

Rylee grabbed her backpack. "You can't go," Kaleb said, taking her by the hand. "This is what they want you to do."

"He's right," Rob said. "Let us take care of this."

"I have a really bad feeling." She placed a hand to her stomach, her eyes shining with unshed tears.

"We'll put in a request to have your mother picked up right away," Jim told her.

"Thank you," she said.

A shiver ran down her spine. "Kaleb, if anything happens to her—it's my fault. Maybe you were right and I should've stayed away."

"They don't know that you're here, Rylee. Brenda only suspects that you're back in Los Angeles. She doesn't know for sure. With your mother in a safe house, she won't have any leverage."

"I hope you're right."

He hugged her. "Everything is going to be fine."

He could tell Rylee wasn't so sure.

"DID THEY GET my mom? Is she safe?" Rylee asked when Jim received a phone call that evening.

"A team of agents went to her house…"

"And?"

"Daphne wasn't there. The door wasn't locked…it looked like she may have been taken—"

Rylee glanced at Kaleb then back at Jim. "Are you telling me that she's been *kidnapped*? That Calderon has my mother?"

She felt like she'd been punched in her gut. It knocked the wind out of Rylee, and she was finding it difficult to catch her breath. She felt her knees shake, threatening to drop her to the floor.

Kaleb pulled her into his arms. "We're gonna get her back," he assured her.

"We have to," she stated. "I can't lose my mother."

He hugged her. "Everything is going to be fine."

"Hey, she's making a call," one of the agents said.

Kaleb's cell phone rang.

"It's Brenda. I'd better answer it."

Rylee stood by Jim, listening.

"Hello…" he said.

"Listen to me," Brenda began. "I know Rolanda Green is with you. It's imperative that you turn this woman over to us or her mother will die. I know you don't want that to happen."

He didn't respond.

"Kaleb…let's not continue this game."

"You'd better not hurt an innocent woman," he bit out.

"No one wants to hurt Daphne Green—they just want Rolanda," Brenda stated.

"Why?" he demanded. "So you can kill her?"

"I was just told to make this call. Look, these are dangerous people, Kaleb. I really don't want to see you get hurt or worse over a woman you care nothing about."

Rylee seethed inside with fury. This woman dared to presume Kaleb's feelings for her.

"Brenda, there's no one with me. I came to California alone."

"I don't believe you," she responded.

"Do you want to come to my room to verify?"

"Listen, there's a million dollars on the table if you give us Rolanda."

"I don't want your money. And I don't have anyone in protective custody. You sent a man to my house and what did he find—nothing. Because there wasn't anyone there."

"Okay…but I'm sure you know where she is. You're the only person Easton would've trusted."

"Tell that snake that I'll be here in two days," Rylee whispered.

"Look, she contacted me, but I'm not with her. All I know is that she won't arrive for another two days," he said. "She didn't tell me where she was—she's not exactly the trusting type."

Rylee gave him a thumbs-up.

Brenda sighed in frustration. "How is she arriving?"

"I don't know. She decided she was better off on her own."

"Well, her mother is being well taken care of," Brenda said. "You should call Rolanda and tell her that. I'm sure she'll make coming to Los Angeles a priority."

"Let the poor woman go. Don't you think she's had to endure enough by not having her daughter in her life?"

"I can't do anything about that." Brenda sighed in resignation. "Easton never should've placed this burden on you. I'll do what I can to make sure nothing happens to Daphne."

"I'll let you know when Rolanda arrives."

"Thank you," she murmured. "Kaleb…"

He ended the call.

"I'm going to snatch that lying witch…" Rylee uttered, her fingers clenched tightly into a fist.

"We know that Brenda's having dinner with someone tomorrow," Kaleb said. "We'll have her followed. I'm sure she'll lead us to your mother."

"I can't wait to talk to that woman face-to-face."

Kaleb sat down beside Rylee, reached over and took her hand in his own.

"They'd better not hurt her," she whispered.

She couldn't bear the thought of harm coming to her mother. A feeling of helplessness once again descended on her. "I could go over to that hotel and force Brenda to tell me where they're keeping my mother."

"That's not a good idea, Rylee."

She glared at Kaleb. "Why not? She's in that hotel room alone."

"Why don't you try to get some sleep?" he asked. "We're going to have a long day tomorrow."

"I can't sleep knowing my mother is somewhere scared. She doesn't deserve any of this."

Rylee clasped her hands together. "All I've thought about is returning to HSI… I never once considered that my job could put my mother's life in danger."

"You can't blame yourself."

She looked at him. "But I am the one to blame, Kaleb."

"So, what are you saying right now? Are you going to give up what you love?"

"I don't know. I'm exhausted to the point that I can't think straight. All I care about is getting my mom back. Once she's safe, I'll sort out everything else."

Rylee rose to her feet and began pacing.

Kaleb made her a cup of herbal tea.

She sipped the warm liquid. "Thanks."

Kaleb wrapped Rylee in his arms, making her feel safe. He was so caring and gentle. She blinked back tears.

"Try to get some sleep," he said before releasing her.

Rylee got up and walked into the bedroom. She left the door between the adjoining suites open so Kaleb, Jim and Rob could see if anyone tried to break into her room.

She got into bed and closed her eyes, praying for sleep to overtake her.

Chapter Twenty-One

Kaleb covered Rylee's sleeping form with a blanket.

She'd fought off her exhaustion valiantly, but sleep eventually won out.

"How long did you work with Rylee?" he asked Rob when he returned to the living room.

"For four years. I always admired her work ethic," the agent stated. "Rolanda and Stuart were exemplary agents. I'm glad she's still alive."

"It sounds like she was well-liked."

Jim agreed. "Everybody liked her."

Rob gestured to get their attention. "Hey, Brenda's making another phone call."

They listened.

"Rolanda's coming to Los Angeles," Brenda said. "I made the call to Kaleb. He said she's not with him, but he expects her to arrive in two days. Calderon, I'm sure when she finds out that we have her mother, she won't waste time getting here. He's supposed to call me when she arrives. Listen… I'll let you know." Her tone grew terse. "Goodbye."

"So now we know for sure that Calderon is involved," Jim said. "Should we wake her up?"

"No, let Rylee sleep," Kaleb responded. "There's nothing we can do right now, so that information can wait until morning."

He yawned.

"You should try and get some rest as well," Rob said.

"I think I will. Wake me if she makes any more phone calls," Kaleb said.

"Will do."

He walked into Rylee's room, eyed her for a moment, then grabbed a blanket and navigated to the chair near the window.

Kaleb sat down and covered himself.

Rylee moaned softly but didn't wake up.

Like her, he was worried about her mother's safety.

Since the very first moment he laid eyes on her, Kaleb had an inkling that Brenda was harboring secrets, but he never fathomed that she'd be entangled so profoundly with the ruthless cartel. Was she capable of murder?

WHEN RYLEE WOKE UP, the room was dark, the only light coming from a lamp in the living room. Something had startled her out of her sleep, and for a moment, she didn't know where she was. She sat upright, then remembered.

Kaleb slept soundly in the fabric recliner across from her bed beneath a light blanket.

She didn't remember falling asleep. Rylee checked the time and saw that it was almost six o'clock in the morning.

She sat there watching Kaleb for a few minutes, briefly debating whether to wake him, but she decided to let him rest. She noted the slight smile on his face and wondered what he was dreaming about.

Rylee eased out of bed and tiptoed over to the door, peeking out.

Both HSI agents were asleep. Jim was stretched out on the sofa while Rob, wearing headphones, was slumped over the desk.

She returned to the bed.

"Are you okay?" Kaleb whispered.

"Yeah," Rylee responded, pulling the covers over herself. "I'm fine."

She closed her eyes and prayed for her mother's safety.

Two hours later, she woke up and noticed that Kaleb was already up. She could hear him talking to the HSI agents in the other room.

She slipped off the bed, grabbed her backpack, and went into the bathroom to shower and change clothes.

She dressed in a pair of jeans and a sweatshirt, then entered the second hotel room. "Has Brenda made any more phone calls?"

"Just one," Kaleb said.

"She called Calderon last night to update him."

"Why didn't you wake me up?"

"Rylee, there's nothing we could've done."

"Graham is on his way over here to discuss the operation to rescue your mother," Jim said. "It's taking place this evening."

"I have to be there when it does," she responded. Rylee wasn't about to hang back—her mother needed to see her.

"I ordered some food," Kaleb announced. "It should be arriving soon."

Rylee really didn't have much of an appetite, but she had to keep up her strength. "Thanks."

Her supervisor arrived thirty minutes after they'd all finished eating.

"What's the plan?" Rylee asked Graham. "And please don't tell me that I have to stay here in this room and wait… that's not gonna happen. I'm going to be with you when my mother is rescued."

"Actually, you'll be in the truck with me monitoring the operation," her former supervisor said.

"Great."

"Is that a good idea?" Kaleb asked. "They're after Rylee."

"I don't care if it is or not," she sniped. "I'm not staying in this hotel room."

Kaleb assessed her. "Just make sure you don't get yourself caught."

Rylee sent Kaleb a sharp glare. "I can take care of myself."

"I'm aware of that," he conceded, "but you're thinking with your emotions right now. This is when mistakes are easily made."

"When are you going to trust me?"

"Trust is not the issue. Rylee, I care about you. I know you can handle yourself, but this is your mother…"

"I can't bear to sit idly by and let something dreadful happen to her. Kaleb, my stomach is tied in knots at this very moment. I'm gripped by a fear for her that eclipses any fear I've ever had for myself. If we're not vigilant, Brenda might just slip through our fingers, and that terrifies me to my core."

"I get it. I really do."

"I've been thinking…"

"About what?" he asked.

"Maybe you should go back to Wisconsin. You have your own company. You should go back to it instead of delegating from here. I really don't want anything to happen to you."

He shook his head no. "I'm not leaving you, Rylee. I'm not going anywhere until I know that you're safe."

She'd had a feeling he'd respond that way, and despite her frustration, she appreciated that she didn't have to deal with this alone.

Rylee sat down with her iPad, planning to bide her time until it was time to leave. She tried to finish the book she'd been reading, but it didn't help. Neither did the television show she'd turned on to try to distract herself. She sought to make the next three hours go faster. The agents were going to attempt a rescue later that evening.

"How are you holding up?" Kaleb asked.

She looked up at him. "To be honest, I can't wait to get this day over with."

"We'll be leaving in about an hour."

Rylee felt her eyes grow wet, and she blinked rapidly. She looked away from Kaleb to hide her tears.

He placed an arm around her. "Don't do that… It's okay to cry. Just don't give up hope."

"I'm not," she responded.

Kaleb held her close until Rylee composed herself.

"I'm okay," she said after a moment. She was relieved not to be alone. "Kaleb, I've put everyone, including my mother, in danger. All I've thought about is going back to HSI, but now…I'm realizing that maybe I shouldn't. Maybe when this is over, Mama and I will leave LA and never look back. You and Nate can help us disappear."

"Right now is not the time for you to make a decision like that," he said.

"I can't keep putting other people in danger. It's selfish."

THAT EVENING, Rylee and Kaleb sat in what looked like a utility vehicle to passersby. Inside, they watched a computer monitor as two undercover HSI agents followed Brenda to a Long Beach restaurant located in the next block.

"She's seated at her table," Kaleb said. "The undercovers are at the one behind them."

"Perfect," Rylee murmured. "Look, she just ordered two drinks. If luck is on our side, she's meeting Calderon."

He shook his head. "I don't know… He's too smart to show up now when a woman's been kidnapped. Especially out in the open like this."

She sighed in frustration. "Who do you think she's meeting, then?"

"Judging from the drink, I'd say Brenda's dinner companion is a woman."

"Poppy...?" Rylee frowned in confusion.

"Possibly. I don't know," Kaleb responded. "As far as I know, there aren't any female lieutenants in the organization."

Rylee sat in the van clenching and unclenching her fists. "You don't know how much I want to go in there and throttle that thirsty little snake."

"Yeah, I do... I'd feel the same way, but I'd restrain myself."

She stood there staring at Kaleb. "That's my mother they kidnapped. You can't make me believe that you'd just sit here if it were your mom or even Nate."

She was in panic mode, and Kaleb didn't blame her. If it were a member of his family, he wasn't sure how he'd react. He was worried about Rylee's mom and prayed she was being treated well. "If it meant a chance of finding where they're keeping her, I'd do whatever I had to do."

"Tell those agents to make sure they don't lose her," she told her supervisor. "I want my mother safe and Brenda behind bars."

"We've got several people in place. Perez won't be able to get away," Graham said.

Kaleb took Rylee's hand and gave it a gentle squeeze. He felt the fear pulsing through her veins. He felt powerless to help her.

Rylee would never recover if something happened to her mother.

Chapter Twenty-Two

A woman wearing all black and walking toward the restaurant caught Rylee's attention. She gasped in shock. "I don't believe it."

"What is it?" Kaleb asked.

"That woman in the black dress is Elena Houston. Stuart's wife."

His eyebrows rose in surprise. "Really? Do you think that's who Brenda's having dinner with?"

"I have no idea…"

Rylee chewed her bottom lip. She didn't believe for one minute that it was a coincidence that Elena and Brenda were eating in the same restaurant.

They watched as Elena headed straight to Brenda's table.

"They seem like old friends," Kaleb said.

"You're right about that," Rylee said. "I think I just figured out who gave Stuart that tip…it was her. It was *Brenda*. That's why he wanted to check it out off the books. He didn't want to implicate his wife's friend."

"Do you think your partner discovered Brenda's connection to the cartel?"

Rylee was still struggling to process her shock. "Stuart must have found out somehow. Maybe he confronted her."

"You've spent time with his wife," Kaleb said. "Did you ever feel anything was off with her?"

"No," Rylee responded. "They were separated at the time he was killed, which came as a surprise to everyone because they seemed so happy in the past. I liked Elena."

"Do you think she'll recognize either of the agents in the restaurant?"

"I don't think so. Elena never came to the job. Stuart said she wanted to keep their personal life separate from his work. It was just a handful of people he ever invited over." Rylee continued to watch the monitor.

"There's a possibility that Elena has no idea that Brenda is involved with the cartel. The woman plays her role very well."

"It's possible that Brenda pushed her way into Elena's life with the intent to get to Stuart."

"Why?" her supervisor asked.

Rylee glanced over at Graham. "Maybe Brenda thought she could buy him. When that didn't work, she set him up."

Kaleb glanced at the monitor. "They're talking about shopping. Guess they're attending a party or something. Sounds like it's on Friday night."

"Brenda won't be there," Rylee uttered. "When this is over, I need to have a conversation with Elena about her choice in friends."

"WE HAVE OUR proof that Brenda knows where they're keeping my mother," Rylee stated. "Look…she just ordered a meal to go. It's not much in the way of evidence, but Kaleb, we need to follow her."

"We have to stay out of sight," he responded.

"You do know they will kill my mom. Unless you really plan on turning me over to them tomorrow, we must get my mom away from them *tonight*." Rylee slipped on a bullet-proof vest and prepared to leave the van.

"Rolanda, you're a civilian," her former supervisor reminded her. "You need to stand down and let us do our jobs. We're going to get Daphne, but we have to do this by the book."

"He's right," Kaleb said. Although he knew if it were his mother, he'd react in the same manner.

Rylee clenched her fist, clearly frustrated. "I still want to be there. I'll stay inside the vehicle for now, but my mom needs to see me after you rescue her. It'll help to keep her calm."

"Rylee…"

"I'm okay," she said.

"No, you're not," Kaleb responded.

Rylee sighed in irritation. "Look, I can't stand feeling so helpless."

He embraced her. "You trust the people you used to work with, don't you?"

"Of course I do."

"Then let them do their job. Your mother is going to be fine." Lowering his voice, he said, "If I have to go in to get her myself, I will."

Rylee met his gaze. "Thank you."

She sat back down in the van.

In that moment, Kaleb realized that Rylee Greenwood had dominion over his heart. He'd fallen in love with her.

Deeply.

Kaleb could barely catch his breath as the truth swept over him. He shook away the emotion that had risen full, profuse and in need of attention.

He looked up to find Rylee watching him.

"Is everything okay?" she asked.

"Yeah," he said with a nod.

"The check's been paid," the agent said. "They should be leaving soon."

"Elena's heading out," Rylee said. "That's good. She doesn't need to be caught up in what's about to happen."

Brenda made a phone call before she left the table with the carryout bag.

"We're only guessing she's going to wherever my mother is being held," Rylee said. "What if we're wrong?"

"We can still grab Brenda and question her about where they're keeping your mom," Kaleb responded.

"We're going to follow her in that SUV over there. Once Brenda gets wherever she's going, we're picking her up," Graham announced.

"I'm sure she'll tell us what we want to know," Kaleb said.

"I hope you're right," Rylee responded. "For her sake."

BRENDA DROVE TO a house a few blocks from the restaurant.

Rylee and Kaleb followed in a black SUV with Graham. Her old boss was careful to stay far enough away that Brenda wouldn't realize she was being followed.

They parked on the next block past the house.

Kaleb could feel Rylee fidgeting beside him. He placed a hand over hers. "The agents are on-site. They're checking to see how many people are in the house."

She gave a slight nod.

He knew it was hard for Rylee to just sit patiently and wait for them to retrieve her mother. It wouldn't be easy for him, either, but he'd learned over the years that there were times when waiting paid off.

"Daphne's there. She's in the house," Graham told her. "It's been confirmed."

Rylee leaned forward. "Can they tell me if she's okay?" she asked.

"They have her locked in a room," Graham said, "but she

doesn't appear to be tied up or anything. There's one guard at her door."

"How many people are in the house?" Kaleb asked.

"Looks like there are two men, your mother and Brenda."

Kaleb wanted to get out of the vehicle to help, but he needed to stay to keep Rylee from taking off and running into the house.

"Why is it taking so long?" she questioned.

"Rylee, you know an operation like this can't be rushed. You don't want anyone to get hurt."

She chewed on her bottom lip.

Kaleb felt helpless. He wanted nothing more than to erase Rylee's fears, but there was nothing he could say that would make her feel any better.

Rylee leaned against him, and her closeness seemed to unlock something in his heart and soul.

RYLEE COULDN'T SIT there any longer. She threw open the door and jumped out of the SUV.

She heard Kaleb exit after her, letting out a curse and grabbing her from behind. "You're going to get yourself killed."

"Let me go!" she snapped.

"No. Not until I talk some sense into you." He turned her around to face him.

"Kaleb, this is taking too long," Rylee uttered. "There are three people in there who have guns. I'm sure my mom is scared for her life. I don't want to prolong this for her. It's a horrible feeling."

"Rylee, I understand everything you're going through right now, but you've got to let the agents do their jobs. We don't want to go in blasting with gunfire. You know that."

Tears slipped from her eyes. "Kaleb, I can't just stand idle. Why don't you trust me? I'm still a very good agent."

"I don't know why you think I don't trust you. Look, Rylee, I need *you* to trust *me*," Kaleb countered. "Being hotheaded like this can get someone killed. Besides, it's best that you remain invisible for now. That's what they want—to bring you out of hiding."

He was right, but Rylee didn't want to admit it.

Her supervisor stuck his head out the window, looking stern. "Get back in the vehicle. The agents are inside the house."

"If anything goes wrong, I'm holding you responsible," she told her supervisor.

Graham sighed. "I understand."

Rylee held her breath as she waited for the sound of gunfire. When none was forthcoming, she asked, "What's happening?"

"Look…" Kaleb said after a moment. "Your mom's safe. An agent is escorting her out. Everyone's been arrested."

Rylee got out of the vehicle once more, and this time she rushed down the street to where her mother was being escorted to a car.

She eyed Brenda, who was in handcuffs, sending her a sharp glare.

"Rolanda…" Daphne cried. "Honey, I was so worried about you."

Rylee embraced her mother. "I'm fine. Are you okay? Did they hurt you?"

"Nobody hurt me," her mother said. "But, Rolanda, you can't be here. *You have to go.*"

"I'm not leaving you, Mama." She turned to Kaleb and said, "This is the man who's been helping me, Kaleb Stone."

Daphne smiled at him. "Thank you for protecting my daughter."

"Mama, we're taking you somewhere safe. C'mon, we should get out of here."

They walked to a black SUV and got inside.

"I can't believe you're here," Daphne said. "I've missed you so much."

"I'm glad to be home."

Daphne's eyebrows drew together. "But that man… Calderon wants you dead."

"Once you get to the safe house, don't call any of your friends—don't call any family, either," Rylee instructed. "One of the agents will bring you some clothes and toiletries."

"I understand, but what about you?" Daphne asked. "Where will you be?"

"I'll be staying at a hotel. It's best that we're not together. I can keep you safer that way."

Once they arrived at a house in Westwood, Rylee escorted her mother inside.

"Let's just leave town, Rolanda," her mom said. "I'll go into witness protection with you."

"I'm out of the program."

"But why?"

"I'll explain later. Mama, you have to stay here until I come to get you."

"I don't want you going after those people."

"It's going to be okay."

Daphne looked close to tears. "I can't lose you all over again."

Rylee hugged her mother. "I have to go. I want to make sure Brenda and those guys that kidnapped you are booked and charged."

"Please be careful, sweetheart."

She kissed her mother's cheek. "I will."

When they were back in the car, Rylee's eyes filled with tears. "I feel terrible. She's been through so much, and now I'm just abandoning her…" She glanced over her shoulder at the house. "I wish I could go with her…be with her after what's happened."

"You haven't seen your mother for a while. Why don't you just stay here with Daphne?"

Rylee shook her head.

"Go on, thirty minutes."

She hesitated before agreeing. "Maybe just a quick visit. But I don't want to miss Brenda's interview. I want to hear everything she has to say."

Chapter Twenty-Three

Kaleb followed Rylee back into the house, wondering if a relationship could really work between them. She could be so stubborn and impulsive at times, giving no thought to her own safety.

"I thought you were leaving, sweetheart," Daphne said when they walked back into the house.

Rylee took her mother by the hand. "We do have to leave shortly, but for now, I'm going to stay here with you and make sure you're all right."

Kaleb watched the two women and smiled. He was glad to be a witness to their loving reunion.

He looked at his vibrating phone. There was a message from Nate. His brother had called to check on their progress.

Kaleb texted him back.

Rylee's mother is safe. Will call you tomorrow.

He excused himself to give Rylee some privacy with her mother.

Kaleb joined the HSI agents in the dining room.

"All this time...Rolanda was alive..." one of the agents said with a shake of his head. "Makes you wonder if Stuart's really dead. You know, he had a closed coffin."

He glanced over at Kaleb, who responded, "As far as I know, he died that night."

"Why did Rolanda leave WITSEC?" the other agent asked.

"Because of a leak," Kaleb stated. "Her life was in danger. She had no choice."

"You a marshal?"

"I used to be. Now I'm in private security."

"Now that she's back, we're not gonna let anything happen to her."

He smiled. "That's good to hear, because I feel the same way."

Kaleb got up and peeked into the other room. Rylee and her mother were deep in conversation. Rylee looked at him and smiled. It made him feel good seeing her so happy. He gave her a slight nod before returning to his seat.

Kaleb wondered if she'd still consider giving up law enforcement now that Daphne was safe. He understood why she felt it was the right choice to make, but he knew she'd never truly be happy. Rylee had said herself that returning to Homeland Security was all she'd thought about in WITSEC.

It was in her blood.

He trusted that she would make the right decision.

RYLEE STAYED WITH her mother until she fell asleep. She sat there gently brushing the hair away from her mother's face and sent up a prayer of thanksgiving. Rylee also felt a certain sadness that she'd have to abandon her dream of returning to HSI. She didn't want to risk her mother's safety again.

Walking out of the bedroom, she said to Kaleb, "My mom's a strong woman. I stayed here because I thought she might fall apart at some point, but she didn't. She's more concerned about me than she was for her own safety."

Kaleb nodded. "Sounds like you two have a lot in common."

"Yeah, I guess we do." She chuckled.

Rylee talked to the agents for a few minutes before telling Kaleb, "Let's get going."

Following her out of the house, he said, "Graham is waiting for us to get there before they talk to Brenda. He knew you'd want to be there."

"That's one interview I don't intend to miss."

In the car, Rylee said, "You do know Brenda's going to want to talk to you when we get there."

He glanced in her direction. "You think so? I can't imagine why. Everything is out in the open now. Brenda needs to focus on getting a good attorney to represent her."

She nodded. "This is true."

"I'd like to know something," he said. "Did you really believe I was attracted to Brenda?"

"Yes," Rylee said.

"What would you say if I told you that the only woman I'm interested in is you?"

"I'd say that I'm flattered, Kaleb." Warmth spread through her body.

"And?"

"And your timing sucks," she responded. "We have members of the Mancuso cartel in custody. Right now, this is where we have to place our focus."

THE TWO MEN who'd held Daphne hostage refused to speak. They sat in interrogation rooms glaring at the agents questioning them.

She and Kaleb stood behind the mirrored window watching as the agents walked into the interrogation room where Brenda sat, wiping away her tears.

"Is Kaleb Stone here yet?" she asked. "I want to talk to

him." Brenda looked straight at the mirror. "Kaleb…I need to talk to you. I have to explain what happened. I was forced into this terrible situation. *I'm a victim.*"

She started to cry again. "I need you to help me. They're gonna kill me, Kaleb. Please don't abandon me."

Arms folded across her chest, Rylee uttered, "She's a great actress. I'll say that about her."

Kaleb agreed.

She gave him a sidelong glance. "Aren't you going to talk to her?"

"There's nothing I can do or say."

One of the agents asked Brenda a question.

"I keep telling you that none of this was my idea," she responded. "It was this guy named Luis Ramon who planned all this. He threatened to kill me if I didn't help him."

"Tell us how Luis forced you to betray the agency you worked for," the agent said.

Brenda's expression shifted, becoming severe. "I want a deal and protection," she stated. "I'm not saying a word until I know that I'll be safe. Luis is a very dangerous man."

"She's got a lot of nerve," Rylee uttered. "After getting two marshals killed…she wants *protection.*"

The agent in the room asked, "You've been declaring your innocence—why are you now asking for a deal and protection?"

Folding her arms across her chest, Brenda stated, "I don't have anything to say until someone tells me I'm getting a deal."

Chapter Twenty-Four

"She doesn't deserve a deal," Rylee said. "Two marshals are dead."

"It's up to the US attorney," Kaleb responded. "If her information can take down Calderon…"

"I know that," she stated. "But I don't have to like it."

"You're not going to believe this," Graham said, entering the room. "Brenda Perez aka Brenda Rivas and Elena Houston are first cousins. Their fathers are brothers, and both worked for the Mancuso organization. Both Brenda and Elena were raised by Raul and Poppy after their fathers died."

Stunned, Rylee glanced over at Kaleb. "Elena's maiden name was Romero. She lied to Stuart about her whole life. It's also Brenda's last name—the others are aliases."

"I'm not surprised," he responded. "I knew Brenda wasn't telling me the truth about her life."

"Stuart must have found out, and that's why he and Elena separated. I'm beginning to think she's the one responsible for his death."

Kaleb nodded. "I agree."

"Do you really think Brenda will talk?" Rylee asked Graham.

Her supervisor nodded. "I believe she'll sing like a bird if she can cut some kind of deal."

"I guess she knows firsthand what can happen to her," she

said. "Brenda would have to be placed in protective custody just to keep her alive. I want to talk to her."

"I'm not sure that's a good idea," Kaleb stated. "You're no longer an agent. We won't be able to use whatever she tells you."

"I just want to talk to her in an unofficial capacity."

Her supervisor agreed, and a few minutes later, Rylee was exiting the viewing area.

Brenda's expression turned to shock when Rylee strolled into the interrogation room.

"You wanted me." Rylee held her arms out. *"I'm here."*

"I was just doing my job," Brenda said.

"I'm sure," Rylee responded, taking a seat in one of the chairs the other agent had vacated. "Now we want you to tell us about this *job*. I already know that you and Elena are first cousins and that the two of you were raised by Raul and Poppy."

Brenda pushed away from the table. "You're right. She's my cousin. Her father was Raul's number one, if you know what I mean. When he died, Elena went to live with Raul and Poppy. I believe she was ten years old at the time. They took me in a few years later when my dad was killed in a car accident."

"So, you decided to follow in your father's footsteps?"

Brenda rested her hands, palms up, on the table. "If you're asking if I had a choice, the answer is no. I never had a choice. Whatever Poppy wanted, she got. It was the same for Elena. Poppy wanted her to marry someone in law enforcement. That was the plan. My cousin never really loved Stuart—it was a job to her."

Settling back in the chair, she continued, "Poppy wanted me to do the same. I was engaged to an FBI agent, but things didn't work out between us. I couldn't marry someone I didn't love. That's when I decided to get a job with the marshals' service. I figured that would please her."

Rylee was blown away by the information Brenda volunteered. Kaleb had assumed she'd keep her mouth closed until she secured some deal. She theorized that it was because Brenda was afraid of Calderon. However, she was most surprised about Elena. It made her wonder how well Stuart had known the woman he'd married. She'd spent time with the couple, and they'd looked and acted as if they were very much in love. Stuart had been devastated by their separation but said it was for the best. He told Rylee that they no longer wanted the same things out of life. That they'd grown apart. When she'd expressed her hope that they'd get back together, Stuart was adamant that he and Elena were headed to divorce court. Now she understood why.

Looking past her, Brenda asked, "Is Kaleb here? I want to talk to him."

"He doesn't want to see you."

Brenda teared up. "I really like Kaleb. I hate that you got him involved in all this."

"No," Rylee responded. "*You* got Kaleb involved when you sent Luis after me. Because of you, Easton is dead and so is John."

Brenda huffed out a breath. "John got himself killed when he confronted me. He accused me of being the leak—Luis is the one who shot him. He killed Easton, too."

"John wasn't wrong about you, then."

"He should've minded his own business. I only gave Calderon your name and where you worked. He's the one who sent Luis." Leaning forward, Brenda said, "Tell me something… how were you able to get away?"

Rylee took a step back. "I've heard enough."

Kaleb was waiting for her outside the room.

"Stuart must have discovered the truth about Elena," she told him. "That's why he was divorcing her. She had him killed, then made it look as if he was the one involved with drug trafficking to divert suspicion from herself." Rylee swallowed her anger. "I spent all this time feeling terrible for this woman, and she's the one who set us up."

"I don't understand why Brenda isn't waiting for an attorney."

Rylee shrugged in nonchalance. "Probably because she's afraid Calderon or Poppy will send someone to kill her. I was told she didn't want one."

They walked back over to the two-way mirror.

"Look, I have valuable information, but I'll only share it if you place me in WITSEC," Brenda was saying to an agent.

"It's because of you that the cartel found out a witness was alive," the agent said. "Have you considered that they will find out where you are?"

Brenda was quiet for a moment. "I'm hoping after everything that's happened, the marshals will put more security protocols in place to keep their witnesses safe."

"Wow…" Kaleb muttered.

Rylee eyed him. "I'm surprised she didn't request that *you* protect her."

He glanced over at her. "Ha-ha…"

"Oh, I'm very serious," Rylee stated. "That woman has a thing for you."

Almost as if on cue, Brenda asked, "I want to speak with Kaleb Stone. I know he's here somewhere."

Rylee glanced over at him. "See…for some reason, she's under the impression that you'll come to her aid."

"Well, she's wrong," Kaleb said. "Easton is dead because of her, and while John and I weren't friends, he also lost his life because of her."

"Hanna Nixon, the US attorney, has just arrived," Graham announced.

"Do you think she's going to offer Brenda some kind of deal?" Rylee asked.

"Depending on the information she gives…it's possible," Kaleb responded.

She folded her arms across her chest. "I hate the idea of her not doing any time in prison, but I understand why Nixon would do it."

"It's not enough to just be connected. Brenda has to give up something solid, like where and when drugs are coming in."

Rylee studied Kaleb. "We don't know if she has that kind of information. I'm not sure anyone would trust her enough to discuss shipments around her. Look how much she's said since she's been here."

The US attorney and a senior agent entered the interrogation room.

"Who's this?" Brenda asked.

"This is Mrs. Nixon. She's the US attorney," Graham said when they entered the room.

"Are you the one who can give me a deal?"

"It depends on what you bring to the table," Hanna responded.

"I have information on a huge shipment, but before I tell you anything, I want to know what you're willing to do for me." Brenda paused a moment, then said, "I can also give you Calderon. That's who you really want, isn't it?"

The US attorney and Graham sat there discussing options with her.

After a moment, Brenda said, "What if I told you that there's a huge shipment of fentanyl and other drugs coming in?"

"You know this for sure?" Hanna asked.

She nodded. "Calderon will be there."

"Do you have a location?"

"It's coming to a home on Naples Island in Long Beach. The house has its own private dock."

"Who owns the property?" the US attorney asked.

"I don't know," Brenda responded. "I assume Poppy does. She stays there sometimes when she comes to California."

"Is Poppy Mancuso here in Los Angeles?"

"She was. Poppy doesn't hang around. She's either leaving or already left." Brenda wiped her eyes with her hand. "That woman only looks out for herself. She'd have no problem letting me go down for this. I have to look out for myself, too."

Rylee glanced over at Kaleb. "She's spilling her guts."

He nodded.

She walked out of the interview room. "I want to see if she's telling the truth, but right now, I'm tired and I need to check on my mom."

They headed back to the safe house.

"Tomorrow, I'm going to Long Beach," Rylee told Kaleb. "I'm familiar with that house."

"I'm not leaving your side, so I'm going with you."

She smiled. "We'll leave after breakfast."

During the drive, Kaleb asked, "Are you still thinking about walking away from law enforcement?"

"Yes."

"I don't think you'd be happy, Rylee."

"You did it."

"And I've had some regrets," Kaleb said. "I've missed it. I didn't realize how much until you came into my life. I've enjoyed being Watson to your Sherlock."

She stared out the window. "How do I keep my mom safe?"

"What about working in another department?"

"I guess I could… I just don't think I'd be happy doing something else."

"You don't have to make any decisions right now, sweetheart," Kaleb said.

Rylee didn't want to be selfish. She had to consider her mother's safety. Perhaps if Daphne decided to move to Florida… Kaleb was right. There would be time to consider her options. For now, they were close to apprehending Calderon.

If she had to walk away from her career as a special agent permanently, she'd want to do so knowing that he was in prison for the rest of his life.

"I'M PRETTY SURE this house will be heavily guarded," Kaleb said during the drive to the shipment drop location the next day. "We're not going to be able to get that close to see anything."

"When Brenda mentioned the address, I recognized it," Rylee responded. "I have a friend who lives across the street from that place. Lindsey. We'll go to her house. I have binoculars in my backpack. We can check it out from there."

"I have a pair in mine as well."

"A couple of HSI agents will go over to talk to Lindsey about the use of her house and to prepare her for our visit," Rylee said. "I don't want her to think she's getting a visit from a ghost."

They rode around until she received a call from Jim. "We can head over there now."

As they returned to the neighborhood, Kaleb stated, "This area looks like a perfect location for bringing in drugs."

She indicated Lindsey's neighbor across the road. "That house has its own private marina," Rylee said. "It can accommodate multiple boats—a perfect way to transport narcotics away from prying eyes."

She drove through a gate and parked beside a white Mercedes.

"Hopefully, I won't shock Lindsey too much when we're face-to-face," Rylee said.

"Tell me about this friend of yours."

"Her name is Lindsey Henry. She's a writer of historical fiction."

Rylee checked out the house across the street. There wasn't much she could see or anything about the house that appeared suspicious.

Wearing a hat and sunglasses, she got out of the car.

"Oh, my goodness," Lindsey exclaimed, hugging her. "It really is *you*. Oh, Rolanda, I'm so glad to see you. You have no idea how I've missed you."

"Let's take this reunion inside the house," Kaleb said.

"Of course."

"Where are the other agents?" Rylee asked.

"They'll be back after dark," Lindsey responded. "They'll bring in the equipment then."

Once they were seated in the living room, Lindsey asked, "You were in witness protection?"

"Yes," she responded. "I'm now Rylee Greenwood. My information was leaked, and someone came looking for me. He's in jail now, so there wasn't any point in my staying in the program."

"How terrifying for you."

"Lindsey, how well do you know the people across the street?"

"I don't know them at all. I've seen a few people over there—I'm afraid I don't even know who owns that compound. I knew the old owners. It's absolutely gorgeous inside," Lindsey said. "There's a private swimming pool in the courtyard. Twenty-foot ceilings, a stunning staircase. There are two spacious suites upstairs with marble fireplaces and four other bedrooms. I did hear that the current owner also purchased the two waterfront homes beside it as well."

"Interesting," Rylee murmured.

"I assume they must use the houses for their guests," her friend went on. "They host quite a few parties, but they haven't been a nuisance. They keep them well contained."

Rylee nodded. "Lindsey, I need a huge favor. Kaleb and I need to do some surveillance. Do you mind if we use one of your rooms facing the house? We'll make sure we're not seen, so you won't be in any danger."

"I'm actually flying to New York in a few hours. I'll be there for two weeks." Lindsey handed Rylee a set of keys. "Stay here for as long as you like. And please, be careful… I can't bear losing you a second time."

She embraced her friend. "I knew I could count on you."

When Lindsey left for the airport, Rylee walked over to a window upstairs and peeked out. "Look who just showed up," she stated. "Elena with her children."

"I guess they just missed their foster grandmother."

Grinning, she turned to Kaleb. "No, they haven't. Poppy's still in town. She just walked out of the house with some man."

"Let me see," he responded, approaching the window.

Kaleb seemed to recognize him instantly. "That's Edward Flores. He's from Chicago." He began taking pictures with his phone.

"They seem to know each other quite well, don't you think?" Rylee questioned. "Look at the way they're touching each other."

"Special Agents Daniel Wallace and Liam Andrews are on the way back here to set up communications," Rylee said after she hung up from a conversation with her supervisor.

"He also reminded me that I shouldn't be involved, despite knowing that I'm not going to walk away when I've gotten this close."

Thirty minutes later, Daniel and Liam arrived at the back door. Kaleb helped them with their equipment.

"You can set up in this room," Rylee said, escorting them to a second-floor bedroom.

"Wow… Rolanda," Daniel uttered. "I can't believe this."

She smiled. "It's good to see you." She glanced at the other man. "You, too, Liam."

Liam hugged her. "Glad to be working with you again."

Rylee stepped back. "Poppy Mancuso is over there with Edward Flores, a drug leader out of Chicago."

They got straight to work.

Rylee gave Kaleb a tour of the house.

"This place is amazing," he said, glancing around. "She has a nice security system as well. Do you have the code?"

Rylee nodded. "Lindsey's ex-husband is a real estate developer. He got the house in Santa Barbara, and she stayed here."

"Ah…"

"Oh, Lindsey said the lights are on an automatic timer. She doesn't want people knowing when she's traveling."

"That's good."

Rylee took him to the second floor.

"You can sleep in here," she said. "I'll take the bedroom next door."

They walked into his bedroom, which faced the house across the street.

"A catering van just arrived over there," Kaleb announced.

"Looks like they're planning a dinner or something," Rylee responded. "Brenda said the drugs were coming in tomorrow night… You know…what if they throw parties on the nights they're expecting shipments? Maybe this is how they distribute the drugs to their buyers."

"That's probably why their parties are so well contained," Kaleb interjected. "They don't want to draw the attention of the police. It's a perfect plan. No one would ever suspect anything."

Rylee stared out the window. "Lindsey just thought they were throwing parties."

She heard Kaleb's stomach when it began to protest. "I guess we should've stopped to eat somewhere."

"I could run out to get something," he said.

"No, you shouldn't be seen. We could have something delivered."

"Maybe we can find something in the kitchen," he suggested. "We can replace whatever we use."

"Lindsey's vegan," Rylee said.

He shook his head. "Naw… I have to have some meat and dairy."

She laughed. "I'm kidding."

They went downstairs.

Rylee checked out the refrigerator. "I can make sandwiches for now. The freezer's full, so there will be something for dinner."

She made a list of what they'd have to replace and left it on the counter, and they sat down along with Liam at the breakfast table to eat. Rylee took a plate up to Daniel, who was watching the house across the street.

"We need to hurry up and get back upstairs," she said when she returned. "I want to see who's coming and going out of that house."

"You're in your element," Kaleb said. "This is a part of you."

"If we can make this bust happen, I'll get my life back."

He met her gaze with his own. "We're doing everything we can to make sure that happens."

She smiled. "You're so sweet. I'm glad you're here with me."

"I wouldn't be anywhere else."

Rylee quickly cleaned up behind them when they finished, and then they went back upstairs to continue their surveillance of the house across the street.

"I've seen several men coming and going, but no Calderon," Rylee said. "Maybe this is another one of Brenda's lies."

"The shipment isn't due until tomorrow night. He might not show up until sometime then."

She looked at him. "Or he may not show at all."

"We'll just have to wait and see," Kaleb responded.

Rylee sighed. If Calderon was a no-show…nothing would have changed. And she wouldn't be able to resume her life with her mother unless they both went into hiding.

It wasn't what she wanted for either of them.

IN THE MIDDLE of the night, Kaleb heard movement in the hallway and jumped up.

Easing his way across the floor, he slowly opened the door.

Rylee was pacing in the hallway.

"It's late," Kaleb said. "Why are you still up?"

"I couldn't sleep."

They walked up to the front of the house where Daniel and Liam sat.

"Everything is quiet right now," Liam stated.

"Were you able to get any pictures of the guests arriving?" Rylee asked.

"Some," he responded.

She returned to the bedroom where she had been sleeping and gestured for Kaleb to join her.

She sat down on the edge of the bed. "I'm still processing that Elena is a member of the Mancuso family. I really liked her."

"I can see how she fooled everyone. Brenda, too," Kaleb stated. "They look and act like the girl next door when they're really a person's worst nightmare."

Rylee agreed. "Poppy groomed them well. She's always carried herself like a lady, but I'm learning she's probably a cold-blooded murderer."

Shortly after 6:00 a.m., they returned downstairs. Liam said, "Looks like Poppy is leaving the house."

They rushed into the room with the agents, watching as a man dressed in black placed two pieces of luggage in the trunk of a car.

Arms folded across her chest, Rylee asked, "So if she's leaving…who's hosting the party?"

"Doesn't look like Edward's going with her, but Calderon and Elena are my top two choices," Kaleb responded.

"Are there any outstanding warrants for Poppy?" Rylee asked Rob.

He shook his head. "No, not in the US, but if Brenda is right about that shipment, we'll finally have something solid against Calderon. The indictments against him and your testimony should keep him locked up for years."

"A life sentence isn't long enough," Rylee muttered.

Chapter Twenty-Five

"There's a florist van over there," Rylee said a few hours later. "They're delivering huge arrangements of flowers." She turned to Kaleb. "Looks like it will be quite the party."

"There's been a flurry of vans coming and going all morning," Liam told them. Jim and Rob had arrived to help with surveillance.

"So Brenda was telling the truth," Kaleb stated.

Rylee walked away from the window.

Liam looked over his shoulder back at her. "We got a big fish. Calderon just arrived."

Rylee rushed over to the window. She felt anger wash over her. "We have to make sure he doesn't get away during this operation. He and Elena can't escape. Our success depends on capturing those two."

Rubbing his bald head, Daniel said, "I'm still finding it hard to believe that Stuart was married to a woman involved with the Mancuso cartel and he didn't know."

"At least that explains the money and drugs they found at his house," Liam stated.

She agreed. "It was all her."

Shaking his head in apparent disgust, Daniel said, "You should've seen the way she carried on at his funeral. She played the part of the grieving widow to the hilt."

"Yeah," Liam interjected. "She deserves an Oscar."

Kaleb peeked out the window. "There she is now…"

Rylee looked to see Elena leaving the house with her children.

They watched the house awhile longer, but there were no movements in or out besides catering staff for the party. Two and a half hours later, Rylee spotted Stuart's widow again. "Elena's back, without her kids… At least they won't be caught up in the bust tonight. They will have enough to deal with when their mother goes to prison."

"And when they find out she had their father murdered," Kaleb said.

"I would love to be the one to put the handcuffs on Elena."

"You'd have to get in line," Jim said. "Stuart was a good man. He didn't deserve to go out that way."

"No, he didn't," she murmured. "Tonight, his killers will be in custody. We'll finally have justice for him."

The guests began arriving around 9:00 p.m. Several came by boat. "We have an agent working with the caterer," Jim said. "She was able to tell us that they're expecting no more than forty guests. She and the owner of the company are about to leave now."

"Good," Rylee said. "Calderon is paranoid and doesn't trust anyone."

"You're right about that," Jim responded. "He doesn't allow any staff to remain—this is the only caterer they use for their parties. The staff set up and leave and don't return until the next day to pick up the linens and equipment."

"Do they have a bartender?" Kaleb asked.

"Probably someone who works for them. They use the same DJ as well."

She paced the floor.

Kaleb took Rylee by the hand and led her out of the room.

"Where are you taking me?" she asked.

"I want you to try to relax for a few minutes. Your friend has a gym—why don't we use it?"

"I know what you're trying to do," she said. "You're trying to distract me."

"I'm not hiding my motives," Kaleb responded. "You're going to work yourself into a frenzy."

"I told you I wasn't the most patient person," Rylee responded with a frustrated sigh. "Calderon and Elena are right across the street—I don't want them to get away. This has to end tonight, Kaleb."

"You've worked with many of these agents and police officers before. You know they're more than capable."

"I know," she murmured. "I'm just a bit on edge. I refuse to go back into hiding. I don't want this kind of life for my mom. I'm going to try to convince her to move to Florida with her sister."

"She doesn't have to go alone. You can work down there. The weather's pretty nice, I hear."

Rylee nodded. "I've thought about it, but the thing is…I love it here in LA."

"Daphne probably does, too," Kaleb said. "You have to consider that she may not want to leave, either."

"I know…" She sighed. "I would just worry about her if she stayed here."

"You'll worry about your mother no matter where she is, Rylee."

"This is true."

Rylee's eyelids grew heavy as exhaustion crept in. The teams were waiting for the element of surprise.

"Okay, we're on. Operation Viper is a go…" Liam stated a few hours later.

Rylee and Kaleb got up and went to the window.

They watched as a wave of police, ATF, DEA and HSI

agents in tactical gear and helmets carrying heavy weaponry moved in swiftly from both directions and turned onto the walkway of the home.

"Police! Search warrant!" one officer yelled as agents banged on the front door, then entered the house.

Moments later, they heard gunshots.

Rylee glanced over at Kaleb. "Who is shooting?" she asked.

"It came from one of the other houses," an agent informed them. He was on a call with the DEA command center analysts, who were recording the arrests and the amount of drugs seized in the raid.

Then there was nothing but empty silence.

Jim looked at her and said, "Calderon was just shot by one of the DEA agents."

"Is he dead?" Rylee inquired.

"Waiting for confirmation."

She stood there, staring out the window. Rylee tried to memorize the face of every person escorted out of the houses. "I don't recognize any of these guys."

The paramedics arrived.

Not too long after, Jim said, "It's not him. Calderon is still alive."

"Is he in custody?" she demanded.

"No."

Rylee released a sigh of frustration. "Where is he?"

"They will find him," Kaleb said.

"Wait…where's Elena? I haven't seen them bring her out yet." Rylee left the window and walked over to Daniel. "Has Elena been arrested?"

"They can't find her or Calderon."

"What?" she uttered in astonishment.

"They searched every inch of the place."

"Did Elena take one of the boats?" Kaleb asked.

"No" was the response.

Rylee walked out of the room, swallowing her annoyance. They were so close to dismantling the Mancuso cartel's hold in Los Angeles. They had to find Calderon.

She returned, saying, "Tell them to make sure they check all three houses once more from top to bottom. If Calderon and Elena didn't escape by boat, then they are hiding somewhere in that house…"

The house must have a panic room. She's still in there. I can feel it in my gut.

Rylee pulled her Glock from her backpack, rushed down the stairs and ran across the street. There were still a few DEA and HSI agents going in and out of the other houses on the property. She found the front door unlocked and eased inside.

Rylee stood in the foyer until she heard the rushed sound of footsteps on the marble floor.

"Somebody's in a hurry," Rylee whispered as she tiptoed in the direction of the sound.

Gun raised, Rylee soon found herself face-to-face with the man who wanted her dead.

"Calderon."

He gave her a sinister grin. "You're a hard woman to kill."

WHEN KALEB WALKED out of the bathroom, he looked around. "Where's Rylee?"

"She left in a hurry," Liam said.

"I need to get over to that house," he uttered. "I think she went after Calderon."

Kaleb checked Rylee's backpack and found it empty, the absence of her weapon sending a chill down his spine. "I'm going after Rylee," he declared with determination.

With a sense of urgency, Kaleb left the house and briskly

crossed the street, his mind racing with worry for her safety. His hand rested on his holstered weapon as he cautiously entered the house.

Kaleb and two other agents canvasing the house found Rylee in the living room with her gun pointed at Calderon while Elena's gun was trained on her. He gestured for them to remain in the shadows for now.

His expression deadly, Calderon uttered, "You have to know I'm not going to let you take me in."

"How do you intend to stop me?"

"He has me." Elena's smile was cold and calculating as she strolled confidently toward Calderon, her own weapon still pointed at Rylee. "Drop that gun...*do it now.*"

Reluctantly, Rylee complied.

Kaleb hoped she knew that he was nearby. That he would die before letting any harm come to her.

"Rylee...that name suits you much better than Rolanda," Elena said with a chuckle.

"Shut up," Rylee said. "How could you do this to Stuart and your children?"

Elena shrugged. "My cousin must have cut a deal. Calderon, I told you that Brenda couldn't be trusted." She shook her head. "I knew she'd try to save herself."

Elena offered her weapon to Calderon. "Do you want the pleasure of shooting her?"

He grinned. "Yes."

Rylee met Calderon's gaze with unwavering defiance. "You better make sure you kill me this time because if you don't—I'm going to make sure you spend the rest of your life in prison."

Calderon's response was abrupt, raising his gun to fire.

But before he could pull the trigger, a gunshot echoed through the room, the bullet striking him in the right arm.

Elena's attempt to escape was halted as the other agent intervened, ensuring that she couldn't.

Rylee picked up her gun and pointed it at Calderon once more, despite agents placing him in custody.

Kaleb stood beside her. "Let the agents do their job."

"TELL ME SOMETHING," Rylee said before she was escorted out of the house. "Why did you do it, Elena? Stuart loved you more than his own life. How could you do this to your own husband—the father of your children?"

"If he'd just minded his own business…" Elena shrugged in nonchalance. "Unfortunately, Stuart overheard a conversation I was having with Poppy. He confronted me, so I had no choice but to tell him the truth. When Stuart threatened to divorce me and take custody of our children, I gave him the false information about a shipment that was supposed to be arriving. I wasn't about to let him take my children from me."

Rylee glared. "You had Stuart killed to keep him from getting custody. You tried to kill me, too."

"That wasn't part of the plan. You were simply collateral damage."

"Oh, I'm going to end up being your worst nightmare, Elena," Rylee stated. "I'm going to personally see that you get what's coming to you."

Elena burst into laughter. "I'm untouchable. You're the one who's going to have to watch your back for the rest of your life. Calderon—"

"Will be in prison for the rest of his life," Rylee quickly interjected. "You need to worry about your own prison sentence. You're about to discover you're not as indispensable as you think."

"I simply came here for the party. There's no proof that I'm guilty of anything. I doubt you're wearing a wire. It will be your word against mine. As for my cousin…well, we'll have to see what happens to her."

Giving Rylee an unbothered look, Elena vowed, "I promise you I won't serve a day in prison."

"Good luck with that," she responded, watching as the agents escorted Elena to a waiting vehicle.

Outside, Rylee turned to Kaleb, hugging him. "We did it. We got both Elena and Calderon… The agents seized nearly four hundred grams of fentanyl. They also found cocaine, Xanax pills and several thousand dollars in cash."

He nodded. "Liam said that arrests have also been made in Arizona and Texas. Brenda's information on that shipment of fentanyl was solid."

"That's great news," she said. "It will take some time for the cartel to recover. Right now, they're in a very vulnerable position."

Rylee felt a sense of satisfaction. Calderon and Elena were going to prison. However she wouldn't be fully satisfied until she took down Poppy, too.

AT THE POLICE STATION, Rylee entered the interrogation room with an agent.

Elena rolled her eyes. "What did you come here for? To try to convince me to talk? Well, you're wasting your time. My attorney should be arriving soon."

Rylee tilted her head. "Elena, this is what I know… Poppy doesn't care about you. She will have you killed in prison, then raise your innocent children, turning them into criminals like she did you and your cousin. *Think about it.* Don't you want to protect your children?"

The arrogance in Elena's voice evaporated. "I have nothing to say."

"Tell us where we can find Poppy. If you tell us where

she is, we can have the children picked up and taken to Stuart's sister."

"Poppy is long gone," Elena said with a smirk. "I called her when the agents showed up. You think you've done something by arresting Calderon—he's not the real threat."

"So the rumors are true," Rylee said. "Poppy is the head of the cartel."

Elena didn't respond.

"So, I guess you know Poppy's already making adjustments now that you and Calderon have been arrested."

"You already have your snitch."

"Think of your son and daughter, Elena. I know you love them, even if you didn't love their father."

She looked away.

"Just so you know, I'm glad that you're finally going to get what you deserve," Rylee uttered before walking out of the interrogation room. "Stuart can finally rest in peace."

"This isn't over. The Mancuso cartel is very resilient."

Rylee paused in the doorway long enough to say, "Oh, it's over for you."

Rylee exited and joined Kaleb and SSA Graham. "Poppy's gone," she stated. "Elena warned her when she was in hiding." She shook her head sadly. "I feel bad for Stuart's children. Poppy will do to them what she did to Elena and Brenda."

"Hopefully, we'll be able to save them before that happens. Kaleb was just telling me about your special task force idea. I'd like to discuss this with you in detail. Now that we know Poppy is the head of the Mancuso organization…we're focusing our efforts on her."

"I'd be happy to discuss my ideas with you."

"You look peaceful," Kaleb said when they left. "I don't know why you're not falling down on your face with exhaustion."

"I wish we could've grabbed Poppy, too, but I'm grateful. At least we've broken off a solid branch of the Mancuso organization."

"And your partner has been vindicated," Kaleb stated.

Rylee smiled. "Yes, but I don't think Stuart will rest easy until his children are with his family. They can't stay with Poppy."

"I guess that will be up to the courts to decide."

She sighed in resignation. "I guess…"

Rylee fell asleep on the way back to Lindsey's house, where they would stay the night.

Kaleb was glad to see her resting. The ordeal was finally over. She deserved this and more.

Chapter Twenty-Six

The next morning, Rylee and Kaleb helped the HSI agents pack up their equipment. After making sure everything was in its place, they left Lindsey's house.

In the daylight, the house across the street looked like it had been raided. Food, decorations and broken champagne bottles were strewed around the yard and driveway.

"That place is a mess," Kaleb uttered.

"Not our problem." Rylee got into the car and turned the ignition. "Let's go pick up my mother."

Daphne was in her bedroom reading when they arrived at the safe house. She rushed over to her daughter. "Is everything okay?"

"Yes, Mama. There was a huge bust last night. A lot of people are in jail, including Calderon, the guy who came looking for me in Wisconsin…and Elena."

"Stuart's wife?" Daphne asked in confusion. "Why was she arrested?"

"She's connected to the cartel."

Her mother looked shocked. "Oh my goodness…"

"I felt the same way," Rylee said.

Rylee walked over to the two agents. "I want to thank you both for taking such good care of my mom."

"Rolanda, it was our pleasure," an agent named Harold said. "Welcome back to the land of the living."

She chuckled. "I'm happy to be back."

"Have you given any thought to moving to Florida with your sister?" Rylee asked her mother when they were on the way to their home.

"I did," her mother responded. "But I think I'd rather move to Oceanside. California is all I know, and I've always loved the beach. I've been looking on the internet and found a house that's perfect."

She squeezed her mom's hand. "Mama…I think moving to Oceanside will be good for you. You won't be too far away for me to visit."

"Are you getting your job back?"

"I have a meeting tomorrow with Burns."

"I know how much you love your job, and you're good at it."

"Your mother's right," Kaleb interjected from the back seat.

She offered him a smile before saying, "Mama, why don't we grab some lunch? After that, we're going home."

Daphne grinned. "I'd love that."

After lunch, Rylee drove to her town house.

"You have a beautiful house," Kaleb said when she gave him a tour.

"Thanks, but I'm going to sell it. It's been compromised. Mama will be living in Oceanside, and I don't need this much house." Rylee gave him a sidelong glance. "I guess you'll be heading home soon."

He grinned. "Are you ready to get rid of me already?"

"No, of course not. I enjoy your company."

"Burns wants to meet with me tomorrow as well," Kaleb announced. "He wants me to come in with you."

Her eyebrows rose in surprise. "Really?"

He nodded.

"Maybe he's going to offer you a job," she responded. "If he does, are you going to consider it?"

"I'd definitely give it some thought."

Rylee smiled.

That evening, they went to dinner alone.

"Why didn't your mom want to join us?" Kaleb asked as they were seated.

"Mama said she wanted to give us some private time," Rylee said.

Kaleb broke into a grin. "I would have to say that I agree with her. Now that Calderon is no longer a threat and Elena is locked up, we can finally have that conversation we've been putting off."

"Can we hold off on that conversation for one more day?" Rylee asked. "Let's just see why Burns wants to talk to us."

She didn't feel they could make any decisions about a relationship until they made decisions regarding their careers first. Kaleb had his own company back in Wisconsin. Rylee had no interest in living there. She also wasn't interested in a long-distance relationship. She was a California girl at heart and had just returned home. She wanted to be near her mother.

"Sure. We can wait one more day."

"Have you spoken to Nate?" Rylee inquired.

"Yeah. He and my parents are still enjoying Canada."

"That's wonderful," she said. "So…if you got the chance to return to law enforcement, what would you do about the company?"

"It's always been Nate's dream. He asked me to be his partner after I left the marshals' service."

"I always thought it was your baby."

Kaleb shook his head. "No. Don't get me wrong—I've enjoyed working with my brother, but Nate was right. I miss being in law enforcement."

Rylee nodded. "I've given it a lot of thought, and the truth is that I can't wait to get back to work. I feel good about what I do, and I don't want to give it up."

"I'm glad you're able to return to your life," Kaleb said. "Most people in WITSEC don't get that chance."

"Trust me…I realize just how fortunate I am."

"I'M SURE YOU have an idea why I wanted to speak with the two of you," SAC Burns began the following morning. "Rolanda… I'm sorry, I mean Rylee. It may take me a minute to get used to calling you that. Anyway, the agency would love to have you back."

"That's great," she responded. "I want nothing more than to come back to HSI."

Kaleb eyed Rylee. She looked ecstatic, and he couldn't blame her. After fifteen months in WITSEC, she was finally able to step back into her old life. He was happy for her.

Burns turned to Kaleb, saying, "I'd also like to offer you a position with Homeland Security. That is, if you're interested. You can work out of the Wisconsin office if you'd like."

"I'm honored," he responded. "I will need to turn over my share of our company to my brother. But I'd like to work here in Los Angeles."

Kaleb saw the surprised expression on Rylee's face and bit back a smile. They talked a little while longer as Burns outlined his full offer, then the meeting came to a close.

When they walked out of the building, Rylee said, "So you're moving to Los Angeles."

"Yeah. I know you don't want to live in Wisconsin."

"But Milwaukee is your home, Kaleb. Burns said you can work out of the office there. You should do what's best for you."

"Rylee," he began with a weighty sigh, his gaze locked onto hers, his emotions stirring within. "I've devoted countless hours to contemplating this, and, honestly, remaining here in Los Angeles is what I believe is truly best for me." His love for her was a wellspring of emotion he could no longer suppress, and he longed to delve into the potential future they could share. "Don't you agree that it's high time for us to have that conversation?"

She nodded. "Yes, I suppose so."

"Do you want to talk now?"

"We can," Rylee said. "Now is as good as any time. I have to say that I still can't believe you're willing to move to California."

"Why are you so surprised?" he asked.

"You never once mentioned leaving Milwaukee. And I know how close you and Nate are—how do you think he's going to feel about all this?"

"I'm pretty sure this won't come as a shock to my brother. He knows how much I care about you, Rylee."

"So, I think it's time you told me about these feelings."

He pulled her into his arms. "From the moment I saw you standing there with a gun pointed at me, I felt a quickening in my heart. The more I got to know you… I didn't want to let you go. The truth is that I can't see my life without you. Rylee, I love you."

She smiled. "I never thought I'd feel this way about anybody. I've always been focused on my career. But then I met you, Kaleb, and I felt safe with you." Rylee paused a heartbeat before continuing. "What I'm trying to say is that I love you, too."

Kaleb's body relaxed.

Rylee wrapped her arms around his neck and kissed him. The hold he had on her waist was gentle and protective. It was everything she needed in that moment.

US Attorney Hanna Nixon walked up to the podium to kick off the press conference. "Today we're thrilled to announce the results of Operation Viper, a joint-agency operation targeting the Mancuso cartel, a South American–based cartel that controls up to two-thirds of the drug market in the United States. This investigation, led by the US Drug Enforcement Administration, has culminated in ten arrests throughout the US, including here in Los Angeles, where ten indictments were filed in federal court."

Rylee glanced over at Kaleb and smiled. She was looking forward to building a future with him. She was free to live her life, and Kaleb was finally free of the shadows of his past. She was also looking forward to working in the Special Operations Division (SOD) of Homeland Security.

"International drug trafficking organizations such as this one bring the pain of addiction and the scourge of violence to the United States," Nixon said.

After the press conference, they walked toward the building on Spring Street. They were soon on their way to the airport.

"How long will you be gone?" Rylee asked in the car.

"Long enough to pack up the house," Kaleb said. "I should be back here in a couple weeks."

"I'm going to miss you."

He kissed her. "I'll miss you, too."

"What did Nate say when you told him that you'll be working with Homeland Security?"

"My brother wasn't surprised at all. He also wasn't surprised that we're together."

She laughed. "I guess he wouldn't be."

Thirty minutes later, Rylee stopped the vehicle in front of the Delta terminal. "Well, we're here."

Kaleb glanced over at her. "I'll be back before you know it, sweetheart. You have to help your mom get settled in Ocean-side, find a place to live and prepare to go back to work."

"I have enough to keep me busy, but it won't keep me from missing you."

He kissed her. "It's just a couple of weeks. When I return, Wisconsin will be my past, and you...you're my future."

* * * * *